The PATRON SAINT of BIRDS

STORIES

(plus two)

Steve Lambert

The PATRON SAINT of BIRDS

STORIES

(plus two)

Steve Lambert

STHRNMST BKS | SAINT AUGUSTINE, FL 2024

First Edition (2020) ISBN : 9798687243100
Cowboy Jamboree Press
www.cowboyjamboreemagazine.com

Second Edition (2024) ISBN: 9798218495305
Southernmost Books
Southernmostbooks.wordpress.com

Cover and Interior Design: Gavin Stephen Lambert III
Front Cover Art: ECrafts, Adobe Stock

Also by Steve Lambert

poetry
Heat Seekers (2017)
In Eynsham (2020)
The Shamble (2021)

fiction
The Patron Saint of Birds (2020)
Philisteens (2021)
Mortality Birds [with Timothy Dodd] (2022)

Table of Contents

For my family

What do a few crimes
matter in a good life?

-Alan Dugan

"Tribulations of Rural Floridians"

Review of The Patron Saint of Birds *by Vern Smith,* *first published in* Reckon Review

There's a fair bit of journalism in Steve Lambert's short fiction. By that, I mean he has real powers of observation when assessing the human condition of the denizens of Sahwoklee County. Or, put another way, he is keenly interested in documenting the tribulations of rural Floridians who have little to lose in such a way as to dignify the undignified.

From the opening story of his latest book, *The Patron Saint of Birds*, Lambert launches into "The Tragedy of Carter Simms," which reads like a deeply informed column in the local newspaper, complete with a veiled prediction that the sins of the father will be visited upon the daughter. But it's the hidden murder mystery about a wife and husband who hate each other in which Lambert demonstrates complete control of his dialogue. It's as much about how characters who make up this loosely connected collection talk as it is about what they say, and clearly, Lambert has been listening. Either that, or he has a lot of imaginary friends from small-town Florida.

While crime is often at the forefront, the fiction is decidedly (and refreshingly) non-genre, something that paves the way in "Tightrope Walker" – the gem of the collection – for the incredibly human take on a man sentenced to house arrest who briefly forgets about his electronic tracking device, crosses the line, then decides to go on the last date he'll go on for a while. For me, it conjured memories of truly great walking stories – such as "Curtis's Charm" by Jim Carroll – while never ever crossing swords.

This is not poverty porn. No, this collection is about understanding what poverty will do to a person, the depths they will be driven to, particularly in times of sickness, and that can include selling one's soul.

At different points in their lives, characters weave in and out of these works – such as Peg Vernon who famously won the catfish festival's wet T-shirt contest every year from 1988 to 1991 – and that gives this collection just the right amount of flow. With pieces written both in the third and first-person, Lambert demonstrates excellent range in terms of storytelling, most notably when he convincingly adopts the voice of a young girl living on an abandoned bus.

Whether it's kids playing a game of William Tell with a pellet gun or a man finding some semblance of peace in drag, these stories often deal with failed relationships, injury, ruined lives, and death. Nonetheless, there are moments of comic relief, lightness, and, dare I say hope. That's not to say hope is always reasonable or even advisable, just that Lambert's characters sometimes have it when they reasonably shouldn't, and that is one but one of the attributes that allows them, in most cases, to survive just a little longer. It's also something that makes them three-dimensional.

Putting together a short-story collection is always a pretty neat trick. They are bound to be uneven. And indeed, some stories here are better than others. However, given the concept-album approach, each piece plays a vital role in driving the concept to its conclusive title track, and that's one of the many traits that makes this book a keeper.

__Vern Smith__ is the author of the novels Under the Table (a payroll heist set on a Hollywood North TV shoot circa 1989) and The Green Ghetto (an urban western). His novelette, The Gimmick—a finalist for Canada's highest crime-writing honor, the Arthur Ellis Award—is the title track of his second collection of fiction, The Gimmick: novelettes, stories, and sketches. He is editor of the crime-fiction anthology Jacked, from Run Amok Books.

The Tragedy of Carter Simms

In a sixth-sense way we knew that Carter Simms would end up in a fix, so we treated him special, like a puppy or a now infirm uncle who'd been cool to us when we were little. We knew he didn't have much time in the clear, was always gonna lose, but it didn't have to go down the way it did.

It's like watching a person rot. In three years' time he went from Stud Number One to limping troll—hunched, black-toothed, yellow-eyed, filthy. You'd see him twitching around town with a toaster tucked under his scabby arm. Walking to the pawn shop. Getting money for more of what was killing him. How many microwaves can one man possibly have access to?

One morning at dawn, driving to work, I noticed something on the shoulder of the road: a person, laid out in the coming daylight, with an old black-and-white TV setting next to him. Carter Simms. He'd just passed out like that. Took a break on the way to the pawn shop and fell asleep.

I stopped and got him up—left the TV—and worked him into the back seat of my car and drove him to his parents' place. His dad walked out to the car and leaned in and looked at his boy, unconscious, drooling, filthy and unaware. "I don't want nothing to do with him. I'm through. Take him somewheres else." I took him to Cynthia's house.

They had a child together, a little girl named Mandy, with her daddy's devious eyes. She wasn't home. I had to get to work. What was I supposed to do? I drove to the Circle K and pulled around back and dragged him out and settled him against the wall. I put a five-dollar bill in his breast pocket.

About a year later, he seemed to get his act together. Got back with Cynthia. Got off the meth. Got a decent job at the Winn-Dixie distribution center. Got his teeth fixed. He and Cynthia even managed to save some money and bought a decent little home in a quiet part of town. But it turned out he wasn't really clean. He'd swapped meth for vodka.

First I saw it on the six o'clock news—then read it in the paper.

He hadn't hit her. The front of the car missed her when he swerved. He thought he was clear, thought he'd done right, but as he swerved, the car fishtailed into the shoulder, and the curled end of his steel bumper caught the strap of her backpack and flung her into the road, dropped her in front of the pickup truck behind him. It all went down so quickly that the old man driving the pickup didn't even know—thought he'd hit a dog. You should have seen the old man's shattered face on the news report. Carter pleaded guilty and because he had so many priors got twenty years.

The other day I saw Mandy, Carter's little girl, at that same Circle K I'd dropped her daddy off at all those years ago. She stood out front, next to a souped-up Mazda too nice for the boy who sat in it, smoking a cigarette and talking, looking tough. As I passed, she watched me with her daddy's bright, conniving eyes and smiled through a swell of cigarette smoke.

A Song for Enid Pound

Frank stuck his hand out the window as he drove and let the wind move it. He liked the peace and quiet of early mornings, and Saturdays were usually the quietest and most peaceful of all. Most folks were still sleeping off hangovers, or just taking their time, savoring the long solitude of it. The stillness of the town reminded him of the movie *The Omega Man:* Charlton Heston driving around thinking he was the last man on earth. This early, everything downtown was closed except Sunrise Diner and the Jiffy Food Store, two places that did not draw crowds anyway; Confederate Park, in the center of downtown, looked like a cemetery. Frank stopped at the Jiffy and bought a twelve-pack of Busch.

As he drove and drank, his mind drifted back to Ben, who he'd spoken to early Friday morning about a couple cases he was working on. Frank had hired Ben, two years before his own retirement, on Delores's recommendation. (Ben was some degree of cousin to Delores.) A good boy, she'd called him, a late bloomer who just needed something to care about. Frank took him on without question, mostly because Delores was, by then, already quite sick, and Frank's anguish and guilt and helplessness had turned him into a pure devotee to his dying wife, something he had failed to be when she was well. Frank's life for those six months had a singular purpose: do whatever Delores asked of him. Ben became a direct beneficiary of this single-mindedness. And, sure as shit, she'd been right; he'd become a passionate and dedicated officer of the law. But, Frank thought, he never did quit being an asshole.

The first case Ben had mentioned that Friday morning involved an old drunk named Kermit, who they both knew, and he'd told Frank the story for amusement. Kermit had robbed Bub's liquor store, armed with only his hand in a brown bag, and made out with almost three hundred dollars. He took the money to the IGA three blocks over and bought two bottles of Night Train and drank himself into a stupor, passing out around back. When he woke, he walked back over to Bub's and tried to buy some Black & Milds and a bottle of Wild Irish Rose with the money he'd robbed from Bub's not six hours earlier. But no one wanted to press charges, not the cashier or the store owner. "When he ain't making poor decisions he's one of my best customers," said Bub.

"This ain't Mayberry," said Ben. "People have to be held accountable. Ain't that right, Mr. Frank?"

Frank said he reckoned. When he was sheriff, he'd always been more concerned with the weight of a punishment, and whether or not it outweighed the crime. Fairness, in his eyes, was most important, and he'd considered himself a fair person.

"One more thing," said Ben. He propped his arm up on the door of Frank's pickup. "Could you keep an eye peeled for Enid Pound?" He explained that she'd reported her husband, Walter, missing a few days earlier and Ben wanted to talk to her. A charred body had been found in an old orange grove in Durdin, a biker town two counties south of Sahwoklee, and there was reason to believe the body was Walter, but they needed Enid to take a look to confirm.

"Don't expect me to go hunting for her," said Frank.

"No, sir," said Ben. He stepped away from the truck and casted the line of a phantom fishing rod.

"Been a while since we got our lines wet."

Eventually, and against his better judgment, Frank ended up in front of the old house on Avenue G, the place where Frank and Delores had spent the bulk of their life together. After her death, Frank had moved into an apartment downtown and let the house and yard on Avenue G go to shit. One of the front windows had a softball-sized hole in it now, and a few loose shingles hung down over the edge of the roof. The grass in the front yard was the color of bad hay and the only green in the yard were the five or six dense clumps of chickweed and clover here and there.

A tall live oak twisted out from the center of the yard, dormant now for winter, but still hung with gray-blue Spanish moss. It was in dire need of trimming. Delores' once impressive knockout roses, which ran along the face of the house on either side of the front porch, had died out finally in the last hard freeze and now looked like bramble. It was hard on Frank, seeing the place like this, everything dead or dying. But he came anyway, because if he tried hard he could see her.

He watched as their phantoms went about the small daily things that, on good days, they had quietly relished. Frank saw himself crouched down in front of the lawn mower, priming the engine, and he saw Delores on tiptoes, arched across one of her rose bushes, clippers in hand, reaching for a stray branch. Now Delores walked over to a young calico, named Fritz, who often wandered onto their property, and coaxed it toward her with a cupped hand. He saw them both at twilight, sitting on the porch steps, surveying the results of their labor and care, he with the rare beer in hand and she with a tall glass of sun tea, front door open behind them, and Tammy Wynette, Delores' favorite, on the record player, whining beautifully about her no-good man. A moment like this could be a whole afternoon for Frank.

Finally, a terse yowl pierced the bubble of his recollection.

He looked up the road and saw Enid Pound picking herself up off the road and climbing back onto her broken-down beach cruiser. Well I'll be damn, thought Frank. This is a providential development. Enid touched her knee and winced, looked down at it. She squinted in Frank's direction and shrugged, as if to say, "So what?" She got poised to pedal away and Frank held up his beer, like a tease, and took a slow sip of it. Enid saw and pedaled toward him.

Still seated on the saddle of her bike, she propped her forearm on the door of Frank's truck. Frank didn't give her time to ask. He handed her a beer.

She put her feet down on the ground, straddling the top tube of the bike, and cracked the tab on the beer and took a thirsty drink of it.

"You're welcome," said Frank.

Enid licked her lips and examined the can. "You don't go in for the high-dollar shit, do you?"

Enid, mantis-thin and wiry, looked much older than her thirty-five years. Her face was small and sharp, and her mouth, devoid of teeth, collapsed in on itself, like a turtle's. Her complexion was sun worn, leathery, and despite the lingering coolness in the air, she wore only a stained white tank top and very short cut-off jeans with an uncountable number of white strings dangling from them. Thin pink flip flops cradled her filthy, narrow feet. At the ball of her shoulder a blurry red rose hovered over the name "Walter," in India ink.

Frank drank from his lukewarm beer. "What you up to, besides falling off that contraption you got there?" He wanted to see if she knew anything about Walter. If she did, she'd say so. She was not one to miss out on an opportunity for some pity or charity.

"Headed over to Fuzzy's. Walter ain't been home for days. Figure he might be there. Good place to start looking anyhow. Not that I really give a rat's ass where he is." She glanced westward, in the direction of Fuzzy's, as if she could see it from where she stood, then looked back at Frank. She drained the beer can of its contents and chucked it into the bed of Frank's truck. "Fucker owes me fifty dollars."

"Why's that?"

"I'd rather not say." She smiled at Frank. "But I'll tell you if you give me another one of them cheap-ass beers."

Frank reached over and got her one.

She cracked the tab and took a long drink of it.

"Well," said Frank.

"They getting warm, ain't they?"

"You know what they say, *beggars can't be choosers*."

"You spot me till I find him?"

"Spot you what?"

"The fifty. Wunst I find him I'll pay you back." She winked at Frank.

"You never did tell me why he owes you in the first place."

"We did veer off track, didn't we?" Enid drained the last bit of beer and chucked the can in the bed of Frank's truck. It kissed a few of the other empties on impact.

"It seems that way."

"Let's just say he lost a bet and leave it at that." The two beers had perked up Enid, Frank thought. She looked less haggard, more youthful.

"Those two beers deserve more of an explanation than that."

"You must be drinking a different beer."

Frank looked over her sorry bike. It had an unintentional camouflage of about six different colors of paint on it: probably an indication of how far removed the bike was from its original and only legitimate owner. In the rare small areas where there was no paint at all, red-brown rust had set in. The seat was scuffed to the stuffing on both sides. The handlebars had no grips of any kind and the tires were bald. He knew that if he gave her any money he'd never see it again.

"Tell you what I'll do. I'll give you a ride," said Frank. "Step away from the door and I'll throw that hunk a shit in the back."

Fuzzy's Bar was nothing more than a skirtless doublewide trailer with a wide front deck on it made of pressure-treated lumber. Frank had often thought that in the event of a category two or higher hurricane the deck would be the only thing left standing. It was late morning and the sun, now in full blaze, had brought the temperature up into the high seventies.

A white and brown pit-bull sat hunched next to the right corner of the deck, chained to a post. Its ears shot up as Frank pulled his truck into the parking lot.

One other vehicle was in the lot, a white F-150 with tinted windows that Frank knew belonged to Roof Maguire, one of the bartenders. Frank got out and unloaded Enid's bike. As he got close to the deck, the dog started prancing and wagging its nub of a tail. He leaned the bike against the deck, and the dog gave a clipped bark. Enid grabbed a metal bowl that was turned over in the mud. The dog watched eagerly, licking its muzzle, as she filled the bowl with water from a nearby spigot. It watched her walk the bowl back and it began lapping at the fresh water before she even had a chance to set the bowl down.

"Surprised the damn thing ain't dead yet. Don't nobody look after it." She shook her head at the dog and walked up the wooden steps.

"Guess I'll go in and have one with you," said Frank. "Ain't in a hurry to rush off nowheres."

Enid walked straight to the restroom and Frank walked straight to the bar. Roof Maguire—tall, lean and dark-haired—had tended bar at Fuzzy's for nearly twenty years. Fuzzy Waid, the owner, had never in all that time found a reason to fire him, and Roof had never found a reason to quit. Roof's mother, a full-blooded Creek from southwest Alabama, had been knifed to death in a bar on the outskirts of Hattiesburg, Mississippi, when he was ten-years-old. Frank remembered it well because the man who'd been convicted of killing her was from a small town in Sahwoklee County, his county—a town with the improbable name of Antarctica. Roof was probably not a bad sort, thought Frank, but he was quiet and solitary and, consequently, he'd never got a proper fix on him.

"What you doing here this time of day, Sheriff?" said Roof in his peculiar half-Indian drawl.

"Throat's a little scratchy."

Roof nodded his head toward the ladies room. "What about your present company? You slumming it or something?"

Frank told Roof to be nice.

Frank walked carefully across the barroom to a table in the corner.

Enid came out of the ladies' room and scanned the area. She saw Frank and walked toward the table.

"First one's on me," said Frank. Enid cleared her throat and sat down.

Frank looked around, taking in details, an old cop's habit. The place had a cave-like quality and smelled of stale beer and old cigarette smoke. It was, Frank thought, what a bar ought to be: a dark, forgiving respite from the harsh brightness of the outside world.

"Guess Walter ain't here," said Enid.

"Nope." Frank took a swig of beer.

"Guess he could be just about anywhere." She glanced toward the front door as if at any second he might walk in, and then looked down at her beer. She turned her brown, too-old face toward the desperate blink and flicker of the jukebox on the other side of the bar. "Why don't you play us a song, Sheriff?"

"Ain't really in the mood for music." Frank motioned toward Roof. When Roof looked up, Frank held up two fingers. Roof nodded. Now that Delores was gone, Frank did not listen to music. Every bit of music in the old house, every CD, tape and record, had been Delores'. She'd loved old country, especially the ladies, singing about how hard it was to be a woman, how hard it was to love their two-timing men. He didn't even listen to music when he was driving around anymore; only talk radio, if anything, and you couldn't really call what he did listening. Instead, he liked to ride with the windows down if it was not too hot or too cold and listen to the sounds outside. Getting rid of all that music was one of the hardest things he did after she died.

Frank drank from his glass and then held it out in front of his face, examining it like some oddity he'd just come across. "Never realized. They got some tee-niny drinking glasses here."

Enid put down her nearly empty glass and flopped against the back of her chair. She glared at Frank. She didn't speak. Roof walked up and sat two glasses down and grabbed the empty ones.

"Roof," said Frank, "how come these here glasses are so small?"

"They're not small, sheriff. You've just got big hands." Roof walked off.

Enid picked up her fresh beer and took a small sip, as if she were consciously trying not to drink it too quickly, and set it back on the table. She reached into the top of her shirt and pulled out a crumpled pack of no-name cigarettes. She dug one out and then fished her finger around in the cellophane wrapper until she brought out a nearly empty book of matches. She paused. "Let me ask you something."

"Shoot," said Frank.

"The fuck you doing here with me, Sheriff? This must be rock-fucking-bottom for you." Her voice was harried sounding, like it had had to fight its way up and out of some deep, craggy place inside her.

Well, thought Frank, she might be sorry, but she ain't stupid.

"Just bored, I guess," he said, trying to keep a casual tone. "By the way, ain't sheriff no more. Wish everybody'd quit calling me that."

"Might help if you stopped acting like one." She lit the cigarette and took a long, hard drag of it, an act that seemed to enlist the whole bottom third of her small, ruined face.

He took a sip of his beer. "Change is hard, I guess." He took another sip and continued his slanted line of inquiry. "Speaking of change, what you still doing with that Walter, anyhow? Bet you could have left him a hundred different times for a hundred different reasons."

"Hell, Frank! I don't know." She held out her hands, palms up, in an oddly girlish display of sarcasm. "Who else is there?"

"All right, settle down," said Frank. He didn't want to scare her off.

After a while Enid got a buzzed, dreamy look about her and stared off in the direction of the jukebox again. "You sure you don't want to play us a song, Frank? I'd like to hear something slow and sad."

"I ain't playing no goddamn music," he said flatly.

She waved a hand at Frank. She looked over at the jukebox and watched the lights dance for a moment. She chuckled, like she'd thought of something mildly humorous, and turned to Frank. "I do hate him, though….I really do. I slam hate the look of him," she said, a dimness coming over her face. "Hates me, too. Might say we was *made* to hate each other. Might say we *love* to hate each other." She chuckled again and brought the cigarette to her lips. She exhaled. "Maybe it's just outta habit. You start doing something, and it's easy enough, so you just keep doing it. It don't have to be right. It's just got to be easy."

"Sounds like a real fairytale you got there, Enid." Frank leaned back and crossed his legs. "Easy is something, I guess." He had a hard time imagining anything being "easy" in relation to Walter Pound. Enid herself didn't look like she'd had an easy go of anything in life, and Frank knew for a fact that she hadn't. "That's a real nice philosophy you got there, Enid, but it don't tell you where Walter is right now, does it?" Frank watched Roof walk up to the entrance, open the door, stick his head out into the sunlight, and retreat back inside. As he walked back behind the bar, he muttered something that sounded like "Stupid dog."

Enid put her full attention on Frank's eyes, stared right into them. "You know something you ain't telling me, Frank? They got Walter locked up or something?" She put her cigarette out in the ashtray.

"What you asking me for? Done told you I ain't sheriff no more." Frank didn't want to say anything about what Ben had told him. He didn't think it was his place to, not anymore. He was just Frank now. Not Sheriff. Not husband. Just Frank. Just nobody.

"Hell, who the fuck cares," she said. She crossed her legs and looked around the room. Her elbows were on the table now and her shoulders curved forward. The front of her tank top hung down, allowing Frank, if he'd wanted one, an easy glimpse of the limp things within. He thought about Enid in relation to Delores. They were like two separate species almost. He took a moment to let his mind drift in vague thoughts of this nature. The sheer variety of humanity, he thought.

Enid leaned in toward the middle of the table. "I got a idea, Sheriff."

"What's that?" said Frank, pulling his mind back into the moment.

"It's just since you ain't sheriff no more—like you said." She looked flirtatiously at Frank. "Why don't you let me take you in the back and loosen you up a little?" She licked her loose, wrinkled top lip. "I'll even give you a discount."

Good God, thought Frank. What a woman. He considered all the times he'd taken her in for prostitution or solicitation. And here she was, no idea where her husband was, and not skipping a goddamn beat.

"That's real tempting, Enid," he finally said. "But I'm gonna pass."

"When's the last time you was with a woman, Frank?" She put her hand on his. "Delores been gone a good long while now…" She started caressing his hand.

He didn't like the way "Delores" lisped out of Enid's lips. He slowly removed his hand from under hers.

She sighed and started for another cigarette. Just then the room brightened up and the front-door hinges screamed. In the doorway stood a paunchy, stooped man in his mid-sixties. Enid and Frank took the time to watch him walk to the bar and take a seat.

She turned back to Frank and stuck the bent cigarette between her lips and lit it. "Ain't Walter," said Enid. She slowly tapped her fingertips against the table.

"Say he *was* locked up, Enid. Say something terrible had happened to Walter. Wouldn't say you looked too damn worried one way or the other." Frank was curious for himself now. He wanted to understand her attitude. He wanted to know how a person could be so unaffected in the face of something like this. She had no idea where he was or what kind of condition he was in.

She took a drag of the cigarette and exhaled to the side. "Guess I can go about being worried without making a big fuss, Sheriff. It's all those years of practice paying off." She coughed and something rattled inside her. She looked intently at Frank. "You sure you don't need to tell me something?"

Frank shook his head and looked at his beer. "Naw."

Enid seemed to lose interest in her talk with Frank. She looked over her shoulder at the man at the bar. She put her smoke out and stood up. "This here's run its course, ain't it, Mr. Frank?"

"I guess it has," said Frank.

Without saying another word to Frank, Enid turned and walked up to the man at the bar and sat down next to him.

Frank wasn't sure why he didn't tell Enid what Ben had said, about the body, probably Walter's, waiting to be identified. Maybe he sympathized with her in some way. He figured that when she did find out, if the body was Walter's, she'd be sad—a little—and then she'd move on. She wouldn't dwell on it. She wouldn't let his death stop her from living her life, as meager a life as it was. Frank reached into his back pocket and pulled out his wallet. He unfolded it and stood it up on the table so that the picture of Delores was facing him. She was standing in the yard of the house on Avenue G, shoeless, her hands on her hips and her head cocked to the side, a big, beautiful smile on her face. A picture of her happy and healthy—before infidelity and sickness had mauled them out of her. He sat and drank and looked at her for a while. Delores, three years gone now, and he still had no idea how to go about the living of his life.

He saw Enid get up and walk halfway to the bathroom. She stopped and glanced back at her companion before turning and walking the rest of the way to the bathroom. The man got up and followed her.

Son of a bitch, thought Frank.

"You gonna let that go on in here?" Frank shouted at Roof.

"Let what?" said Roof. "I ain't seen nothing." Roof smiled and stuck his hand in his pocket.

After about fifteen minutes, the man reappeared and took up his seat at the bar. Shortly after, Enid came out and walked over to the jukebox. She looked at Frank and put a dollar bill in the slot on the jukebox and picked her songs. While she was selecting her last song the first one came on. It was Willie Nelson singing, "Hello Walls."

Enid walked backward a few steps, looking at Frank, winked, then turned around and headed back to her spot next to the paunchy old man, where a drink waited for her.

She did not sit down. She stood and rocked back and forth to the music.

Frank looked down at Delores with that teasing, sexy smile on her face. He decided he'd slowly finish his beer and leave, but after Willie finished up the next song that came on was Tammy Wynette singing, "I Don't Wanna Play House," a song that Frank knew he could not sit through.

He drained his beer, put his wallet back in his pocket, slowly stood up and walked to the other side of the small table and picked up the chair Enid had sat in. He carried it across the room and held it up over his head and brought the seat of it down on top of the jukebox. Glass shattered and flew. The lights on the jukebox blinked erratically. He swung the chair down onto the jukebox two more times until, finally, Tammy purred, "…daddy said goodbye," and the whole thing slurred to a stop.

War In Sahwoklee

Charlie Millsap watched the TV reporter point at shaky video footage of a tower of blooming smoke and call it a *mushroom cloud*. Charlie didn't normally watch the news, but he sometimes caught the end of it before *The Lone Ranger* came on. The news anchor, whose accent was like no one's Charlie was used to hearing in real life, said that the bomb had been tested in Nevada, and he talked about an *arms race* and something called *The Cold War*. "The Cold War," Charlie said. He liked the sound of it. He pictured two opposing lines of men in a snowy field, rifles trained on each other in a frozen stalemate.

The weatherman came on next and began talking about an approaching tropical storm and Charlie lost interest. He didn't like to know the weather ahead of time, and he felt like he knew all there was to know about tropical storms. A change of weather, to Charlie, was something to be relished and experienced in the moment. He decided he didn't want to watch *The Lone Ranger*. All this talk about war had put him in an adventurous mood. He got up from the living room floor and turned off the small black-and-white TV and walked over to the window that opened to the front yard.

Charlie's brother-in-law, Redge Nix, was out working on a car under a huge gnarled oak tree. Charlie's big sister, Ida, had told him that the tree was over 300 years old, and that Hernando Desoto himself had used it as a landmark on his explorations. She'd point to the x-shaped gash in the tree. "See there? That's a mark he made so he knew where he'd already been." He didn't believe her, but he liked thinking about it that way, and he'd sometimes pass on the lie to other kids.

"Redge!" Charlie shouted from the window.

Redge stuck his head out from under the hood of the beat-up car.

"What? Breakfast ready?" He squinted his black eyes up at Charlie. Redge always got up in the morning and went about his business and didn't eat anything until someone, usually Ida, had made him something. Charlie, on the other hand, liked to feed himself, and he liked cooking. Not long ago, Ida had shown him how to make grits and he made them himself every chance he got. He could make oatmeal, too, but he didn't like oatmeal as much as he liked grits.

"Nah. Just seeing if you was still out there working on that car."

"Hell's it look like, boy?" He ducked his head back under the hood.

"I guess I'm a go to the liberry and try and look at books on nukaler bombs."

Redge waved a ratchet in Charlie's direction.

Charlie put a pair of sneakers on and then went into the kitchen and took an apple from a bowl on the dinner table. He stood there and rubbed it on his shirt for a while. It was warm and breezy outside and Charlie decided he'd walk instead of riding his bike. It was Saturday morning and, despite the oncoming storm, it felt to him like he had all the time in the world. Ida came shuffling into the kitchen.

"You fixing to go someplace, little brother?" She yawned.

"I'm a head over to the liberry." He took a bite of the apple. It was warm inside, and soft. He didn't like Macintoshes that much, but it was the only variety of apple they ever had.

"What for?" Her house slippers made a scratchy sound against the linoleum floor as she walked over to the sink and began filling a pot with water.

"Books on nukaler bombs and whatnot." He tried to say it like he was already an expert on the subject. The word "whatnot" seemed to him like a nice touch. "They got these mushroom clouds that they put out on you," he continued.

"Be careful crossing First Street." She skidded over to where Charlie was standing and mussed his hair and flashed a crooked smile down at him. Ida was eighteen-years-old and had already amassed considerable responsibility for herself. She had a two-year-old son with Redge (the boy's name was Lucas and he had purple-black hair like his daddy and a one-sided smile like his momma) and she had been taking care of Charlie ever since their mother had died of cancer three years back, six months after her diagnosis. Her body had been "riddled with cancer." Their pa was still living but nobody knew where he was. Ida kept house and rode a bus into Cuba City every weekday and put in about sixty hours a week at the Okay-Havana cigar factory. Her husband, Redge, worked intermittently, on people's cars, and in the fall he traveled to Michigan with his brother, James, who operated his own harvesting company, and picked apples for two months.

"Oh, hold up a sec!" Ida skittered out of the kitchen and then came back with a half-dollar coin. "Pick up a quart of milk on your way home. You can keep what's left of it, but don't tell your no 'count brother-in-law." Charlie knew that no 'count meant something akin to lazy, but worse. A no 'count, as Charlie would have put it, was someone who enjoyed being lazy. He thought that matched up pretty good with Redge. "Cruel some bitch" was something else he'd heard folks call Redge. Cruel some bitch, in Charlie's mind, meant mean and filthy, like a mistreated dog. Cruel some bitch, coupled with no 'count, meant lazy, mean and filthy. Charlie thought that that was one of the worst combination of traits a person could have.

But what bothered Charlie the most was that he'd heard people refer to his pa, "Charlie Bill" Millsap Sr., as no 'count. In the beginning, he'd heard it from his momma's mouth, and he'd heard it from Ida. But he'd also heard Redge call his pa no 'count, which didn't seem right, because of the two, Redge had to be the bigger no 'count. He didn't like his pa being lumped into the same category as Redge, but it seemed like folks did it quite a lot. He figured if his pa and Redge were no counts then he probably was too, or would be once he got older. It was probably something inescapable, like your eye color or hair color, passed down from pa to son. Redge's pa and Charlie's pa's pa must have been no 'counts too. This made Charlie try to be nice to

Redge, made him try small talk with him even though he never got very far with it. They were both, he figured, assigned to the same no 'count fate, so he had to at least try to get along with him.

Charlie put the coin into his front pocket and started thinking about what he might do with the dime he'd have left over after buying the quart of milk.

Redge was still leaned into the hood of the car when Charlie got out into the front yard. He thought it looked like his uncle was being eaten by a big yellow metal creature.

"See ya, Redge."

Redge moved out from under the hood and stood next to the car. He was a short, skinny man, his shoulders sharp and bony. The skin of his hands, now smeared with car grease, was deep red. His knuckles always had cuts and scrapes on them and his fingernails, bitten down past the tips of his fingers, had a permanent filigree of crud and grime around their edges. He pulled his black mesh cap off his head—the letters C-A-T printed across the front of it in yellow—and set it back down on his head in a more crooked position. Charlie knew that CAT was short for Caterpillar. It seemed like every man he knew had the same greasy old baseball cap. He couldn't recall ever having seen a brand new one. He wondered how that could be. He figured one day he'd have a shitty old CAT cap too.

"Where you headed ta?"

"I done told ya—to the liberry."

"What for? Ain't like you can read." He smiled impishly and revealed the whitest and biggest teeth Charlie had ever seen. At night Redge put his teeth in a clear glass he kept by the bed where they sat submerged, like some rare clam species, until the next morning. One time, when Redge and Ida were still asleep, Charlie crept into their room and took Redge's teeth out of the glass and farted on them and then put them back. He waited all morning for Redge to say something about how something didn't seem right about his teeth, but he never did.

The traffic was heavy on First Street, just as Ida had predicted. Charlie had to wait a few minutes to cross, and when he did finally cross, he had to run at top speed across the four lanes. He hung a left when he got to the other side of the street and walked two blocks down to the theater. The marquee was blank and the theater looked closed. He shrugged it off and walked the rest of the way to the library. Once he was two blocks away from the library he noticed many cars parked alongside the road on both sides.

Outside the library, in open daylight, were several rows of long tables, like the ones they had in the lunchroom at Charlie's school. The tables were stacked high with books. Hung over the front door of the library was a large plastic sign that read "Friends of Sahwoklee Public Library Book Sale!" The sign billowed or wagged every few seconds. A man holding a ladder stood next to the sign.

Charlie walked onto the front lawn of the library and over to where the tables of books began. Most of the books didn't interest Charlie. On one long table were lots of cookbooks and Manuals on how to fix things. Another table was piled high with westerns and romance novels. He liked the pictures on the covers of the westerns but wasn't that interested in what he imagined was inside of them.

A woman he knew to be one of the librarians walked up to him and asked if she could help him find something in particular. She had a large cardboard box in one hand.

"I'm looking for books on nukaler bombs and whatnot," he said in his expert voice.

"That's a bit grim, don't you think?" The librarian set the box on the table and bent forward with her hands on her knees. Charlie thought she was very tall for a woman. He thought she was pretty too. He liked the clean, crisp, sound of her voice and he liked the makeup she wore on her face. He wasn't used to seeing women wear makeup. He didn't know much about the librarian other than her name, Ms. Iris Kelly, and that she was what a lot of folks in Sahwoklee called a Yankee. He also knew that she wasn't married, which from what he had gathered, had something to do with her being a Yankee. He'd heard Ida and her best friend Millie Thornton talking one time not long after Ms. Kelly had first arrived in Sahwoklee, and Ida had said, "Wonder why she ain't married yet?" and Millie had said, "I don't know, exactly, but she *is* a Yankee," and Ida had said "Oh," in a tone that seemed to indicate that that explained it to some degree.

"It is a bit grim," said Charlie. He didn't know what the word meant, but he liked the tough sound of it. "They was talking about it on the news this morning and I got innersted.

They was talking about hydergin bombs and they showed some of them mushroom clouds. You ever see one of them?"

"I've seen pictures."

"I'd like to see some of them pictures."

"Well, there's a table over here that has some science-related books and some history books." She walked over to a table and started shuffling books around. Occasionally, she distractedly glanced around.

"We've got to get packed up before the storm rolls through."

"You got plenty of time," said Charlie. "I know about tropical storms and hurricanes and all that."

The librarian smiled at him. Charlie smiled back and patiently stood next to her while she searched the stacks of books. She smelled good to him. He moved closer.

"Here's a book about World War II. *The Pacific Theater.* It has a section on the bombing of Japan—Hiroshima and Nagasaki."

"Does it got pictures of it?"

She opened the book and after some flipping of pages she showed him a full-page black-and-white picture of a mushroom cloud.

"Those are them. How much is it? All I got to spend's a dime."

"A dime will do."

The lady took his fifty-cent piece and gave him forty cents in change.

"You're not worried about the tropical storm?" she said, smiling.

"Naw." He gripped his new book tightly and glanced up the road.

She straightened up and crossed her arms and surveyed the area with a bunched up brow. "Well, be careful. It's already getting very windy and it should be raining hard by early afternoon."

"Yessum," said Charlie. He thanked her and walked off staring at the front cover of the book, a picture of a bent-over group of soldiers running up a beachhead towards some palm trees.

While Charlie walked to the grocery store he held the book opened to the page with the picture of the exploding bomb on it. It was an aerial photograph taken from a good distance. The cloud was so much bigger than everything else. Even the buildings he'd seen in pictures of places like New York City and Chicago weren't as big as this cloud of smoke. Charlie would look up periodically to make sure he didn't walk into anything. When he got to the grocery store he closed the book and put it under his arm and went inside.

Mr. Clemmons, the store owner, was sitting on a stool behind a counter. He glanced over the top of a newspaper and watched Charlie walk by.

"Mornin, Charlie."

"Mornin, Mr. Clemmons."

Clemmons was long and lean and had a full head of beach-sand colored hair.

Charlie walked to the back of the store, to the refrigerated section, got a quart of milk, and then walked back to the front of the store.

"That a be forty cent."

Charlie handed the coins to Mr. Clemmons.

"What's that you got under your arm there?" Clemmons put his arm on the counter and leaned towards Charlie.

"It's a kind of history book with a section on bombs in it."

"Oh," said Clemmons. "What kind a bombs?" Clemmons was being nosy, but it was a slow day and he was a curious man. Clemmons asked a lot of questions of people, but he wasn't gossipy. He asked questions, got information, and there it stayed. He didn't pass any of it on to other folks, and he didn't entertain questions from anyone else about things he'd discussed with other people. Consequently, people would go to Clemmons to get things said, to unburden themselves. In fact, Charlie was used to going to the grocery store and having to wait in the back, by the comic books, while Clemmons listened to some poor old gal sob her heart out about something or other while he patiently listened.

Charlie opened the book to the page with the picture of the mushroom cloud on it and held it up to the man.

"I know that picture." He took the book and held it up to his bespectacled eyes. "Yes sir…seen that one before."

"Lady to the liberry said it was over in Japan or China sommers."

"That's right, Japan." He put the book down on the counter. "It's a sad thing, for sure. All those innocent folks. Ended that war, though, they say. Brought it right to an end. Still…a life is a life."

Charlie took the book off the counter and put it back under his arm. He asked Clemmons for a bag and he grabbed two brown bags from a rack and put one inside the other and then picked up the quart of milk and put it inside the bags. He curled up the tops of the bags into a handle.

"Best not take too long getting home. These bags'll soak through eventually."

"Was you there, Mr. Clemmons? In that war?" Charlie figured Clemmons was old enough to have been in a war.

Clemmons set the sack down on the counter.

"No sir. I wasn't. But my brother-in-law, Cal, Tank's daddy—he was in it. Not in Japan, though. He was in France during the war. Normandy."

"They drop one of them bombs on France?"

Clemmons took off his reading glasses and gave Charlie an incredulous look. Charlie looked around self-consciously.

"France was an ally, son. We didn't *bomb* France."

Clemmons looked out the window. "Normandy was no picnic, though. Cal didn't come back right." He looked down at the boy. "War ain't nothing to make jokes about."

"I wasn't joking about it." Charlie grabbed the bag off the counter. "I'm serious about wars and bombs and stuff."

Clemmons sat down on his stool and picked up the newspaper and whipped it into the proper v-shape.

Charlie could see his front yard from a block and a half away, and he saw Redge leaning against the big oak tree in front of the car. The wind picked up. Redge had his CAT cap on backwards and he looked like he was talking to someone.

As Charlie approached he watched a little tornado of leaves and debris work its way through the front yard. It crashed into the back end of the car and then died. When a particularly strong gust of wind blew, Redge casually set his hand over his cap until it subsided. Charlie got to the edge of the yard and saw that Redge was talking to Tank Renner, Clemmons' nephew. He thought that was a coincidence and got an urge to say so but thought better of it. He knew Redge would only make fun of him somehow if he did.

Charlie didn't know what was wrong with Tank, but all the kids he knew always called him things like "retarded" and "abnormal." Adults used slightly less offense words like "handicapped" and "disadvantaged." He didn't know how old Tank was but he was pretty sure he was a young adult. Tank didn't do much talking, but he could understand what people said. He rode a red bicycle around town and did mostly normal stuff, but he did walk sort of funny and one of his eyes seemed like it was always leaping around in its socket.

Charlie usually tried to be nice to Tank, but it wasn't easy. There was something a little scary about him, unpredictable, like a spider. Plus he was bigger than most people Charlie knew. Charlie felt jumpy around Tank, always on guard. Still, Charlie said hi to him when he saw him and didn't throw things at him like some of the other kids.

When Redge noticed Charlie walking up, he took off his yellow cap and smoothed back his greasy purple-black hair.

"There he is! We was waiting on you, me and Tank was." He flopped his cap back on his head. Redge's white t-shirt had grease stains and black finger- and handprints all over it.

"You was?"

"Yep. What's at you got under your arm?" Redge snatched the book out from under Charlie's arm and started flipping through the pages with his black and red hands.

"You gonna dirty up my book I just bought!" Charlie put down the sack with the quart of milk in it.

"Waste a money for somebody can't read a lick." He got to the page with the picture of the mushroom cloud and pressed the palm of his hand down flat on the page and smeared it around. "Oh no! I messed up one a the pitchers!"

Charlie went to snatch the book away from him but Redge held it up in the air out of his reach.

Tank, standing next to the hood of the car, made a sound almost like a dog's bark.

"You ain't supposed to make jokes of the war!" said Charlie.

Redge pretended to throw the book and laughed.

Tank barked and walked in tight little circles now.

"Quite your yapping, retard!" said Charlie. He felt bad right away for saying it, especially after talking with his uncle, Mr. Clemmons.

Tank stopped and got quiet. Redge threw the book at Tank. The book bounced off Tank's chest and hit the ground. Charlie ran over and picked it up.

"Sorry for calling you a name." He smiled at Tank. Tank did not respond.

Charlie looked over at Redge. He wanted to hurt him somehow. "Asshole!" he said. He knew he'd pay for it later, but he didn't care. He ran towards the front door of the house.

"You better run off, you little shit!"

Charlie put the quart of milk in the icebox and then ran upstairs into his room and shut the door. He set the book down on his desk and examined it. The cover wasn't too messed up. He took an old t-shirt and rubbed at the greasy spots. They came off easily. He opened the book to the page with the mushroom cloud picture on it. He rubbed at it with the t-shirt. "Damn no 'count asshole," he said. Some of the grease came off, but not all of it. He kept at it and tried to think of something he could do to Redge. He wondered if maybe he could get Tank to beat him up. "Probably not," he said out loud. "He's too kindhearted." Charlie stopped working on the soiled picture and walked over to his bedroom window.

Redge and Tank were still in the yard, but now Redge was sitting in the driver's seat of the car with the door opened and Tank was standing on the front bumper of the car. Charlie couldn't figure out what they were doing so he kept watching. He opened his window and tried shouting down at them but they couldn't hear him over Redge revving the engine.

Redge quit revving the engine and yelled at Tank, "Go on ahead! Go on, boy! Just the way I told ya!"

Tank unzipped the front of his jeans and pulled it out and then looked up towards the top of the big oak tree and closed his eyes. His shoulders twitched and he opened his eyes and a thick golden stream of piss came down on the radiator of the car.

"Aim it! Aim it over to where I showed you!" said Redge and Tank complied, training the stream down into the dark center under the hood of the car.

Redge revved the engine and Tank screamed.

Tank was rolling on the ground in front of the car, moaning, his pants still undone. Redge shut off the car and got out and stood next to Tank. Overcome with joy, holding his yellow cap in his hand, his eyes alternately wide and narrow, he cackled, his hands resting on his knees, then grasping his greasy head, his back bowed and feet wide, convulsing with a perverse pleasure at what he'd done to Tank. A strong wind came up quick and raised the greasy flap of black hair on top of his head.

Tank got up and fastened his pants.

"Well," said Redge, once he stopped laughing. "I think you fixed it for me, Tank. Them plugs weren't firing quite right before, but they is now!" He broke out in a raunchy laugh and then stopped after a few seconds. He put his hat back on.

Charlie called down to Tank.

Tank and Redge both looked up at Charlie standing at the window.

"Beat his ass, Tank! Beat his ass!"

Tank looked over at Redge.

Redge held his hands out. "Don't scare me like at! I'm shaking in my boots!" He laughed some more.

Tank walked up to Redge and grabbed him around the neck. Redge made a clucking sound in his throat and swung his arms around and then grabbed Tank's hands but couldn't loosen his grip. Tank brought Redge's face down to where his piss puddled on top of the car's air filter cover. He rubbed the side of Redge's face in it. Redge let out a kind of squawk and moved his head back and forth in an effort to get out of Tank's grip, but he only made it so that more of his face got coated in Tank's urine. Finally Tank lifted Redge's head and hit it hard on top of the car's radiator. He paused, as if considering what to do next, then did it two more times and let go of Redge. Redge didn't move. Tank unhooked the brace holding up the hood of the car and he slammed it down on Redge's upper back. Tank took a step back and looked at what he'd done.

The wind bullied some leaves loose of the high limbs of the old oak tree. The leaves rained down on the section of the yard Tank stood in. Every few seconds a large rain drop popped against the hood of the old car. Tank looked up at Charlie. Charlie was motionless too. The screen door on the front porch slammed and Ida walked out into the yard. Her hair was damp and she wore a pink bathrobe. Charlie could hear baby Lucas inside crying.

"What the world's going on out here?" She put her hands up to her eyes and squinted, even though the sun was now completely behind dark grey clouds, and she walked over to where Tank stood. she kept one arm clamped down over the front of her robe.

Tank pointed at Redge as if pointing at a mess he'd made.

"This a joke or something?"

Tank kept pointing.

She picked up the hood and engaged the brace. "Redge…Redge…" She poked a finger at Redge's side. He didn't move. She put her hand on his shoulder and his body slid down the front of the car, as if he had been released from its grip. His yellow cap somersaulted off his head unleashing a fan of black hair. A quick gust of wind picked up the cap and tossed it into the gutter where the yard met the road.

Ida looked over at Tank again. Tank pointed up at Charlie's window.

"What you doing in that winder, boy?"

"Nothing."

"You get that milk I asked you to?"

"It's in the icebox."

She looked down again at her husband who was still lying in front of the car. The car belonged to a man named Jasper Talbert, a good friend of Redge's brother, James. He'd hired Redge to fix it as a favor to James. James had asked all his friends to throw some mechanic work Redge's way because he knew Ida was struggling to make ends meet, and he knew Redge was too lazy and proud to ask for himself.

"I guess you'd better get away from that winder, Charlie. Go inside and give Lucas some a that milk you bought. You two stay inside for a little while. Sky's fixing to open up." She watched the window until Charlie closed it and disappeared.

When Charlie turned from the window he saw Lucas standing in the doorway of his room. His cheeks were wet but he wasn't crying anymore. Charlie picked him up and sat him down on his bed and handed him a green plastic army man the size of a small bird. Lucas immediately put it in his mouth and started gnawing on it. Charlie walked over to his desk where the book lay open, one of Redge's black fingerprints still smeared over the top of the mushroom cloud. He picked up the old t-shirt and went to work on it.

Tightrope Walkers

Lucien primes the engine and watches a slug of sweat glide down his shin and break against the ankle bracelet. This is a good, normal thing to do, he tells himself. The edger starts on the third pull. He imagines taking a step over the invisible line, and them coming for him, sirens ablaze—maybe not ablaze, but coming, nonetheless, and driving him south, to Cooper Correctional. He stands revving the engine, deciding what side of the yard to start on when he notices someone coming up the sidewalk. It's Peg Vernon. Beautiful, sweet Peg. Right on time Peg. He cuts off the edger and walks to the middle of the yard and waves a hand.

"Lucien Nix," she says. "I'll be damn." She acts surprised to see him, though she is not. She's been waiting at the street corner for what she thought was the right moment. She looks over the yard with her hand over her eyes for the sun. "You missed some spots with the mower over there." She points.

"Yeah, I know. I was just gonna hit those with the trimmer," he lies. I'm a big liar, he thinks.

She is wearing a sheer, billowy, cream-colored blouse, tucked into brown corduroy pants, and brown desert boots. Her long blond hair is in one fat braid down the middle. This is her, he thinks, seemingly unchanged over the years.

"How did I know it was you, Peg? You look different grown," lying again.

She glances down, as if to remind herself of what she looks like, smiles. "It's been a while, hasn't it—since high school?"

"Since Randall Ginny's graduation party. Ninety-three."

She nods, smiles again, tries not to look at the thing on his ankle.

"Where you headed?"

"Walking to town. Job hunting."

"I remember when you worked at Dino's."

"I still did, until a week ago. It closed down."

"Dino's closed down? Man, I made out with Claudia Nolan in the parking lot of Dino's. She let me touch her boob."

"Many a boob was handled at Dino's—that's for sure."

"Wish I could come along with you. Keep you company."

"Why can't you?" She acts as if she doesn't know the answer.

He points down at the bracelet.

"Shit." She walks forward, into the yard. She squats down and looks at it, touches it, cups it with her hand. It feels warm. She stands up, crosses her arms and clicks her tongue.

"House arrest, huh? What the hell for?"

"I'd rather not say."

"Well…" she claps her hands against her legs.

"I got an idea. Why don't you go and do your job hunting and come back by after. I'll be done with the yard then, and we can sit inside and catch up. I'll tell you all about it."

"Where's your momma? She in there?" Peg looks toward the house. When Peg was about five, Lucien's mother spanked her for picking a lemon out of Lucien's granddaddy's grove. "It's stealing, even if it's only one," she'd said as she laid into her in the front yard, Lucien, seven-years-old, standing nearby. It may not have been the cruelest thing that ever happened to Peg, but it was demeaning and unnecessary and soured Peg on Lucien's mom. She never did forgive her for that. Her hand reaches into her back pocket. She pulls out a black ink pen and hits it against the palm of her hand.

"Naw, she's gone. Out of town for a week. Visiting a cousin, some gal she grew up with. Might not actually be her cousin. She's mellowed over the years." The last bit is another lie, she'd actually gotten worse.

"What happens if you leave your house?" She points at the bracelet. "What does it do?"

"Alerts the police, and they come looking for me."

"Does it tell them where you are?"

"No. Just that I'm not home."

She nods and looks up the road.

"I'll come back by after."

Lucien climbs out of the bathtub and looks into the mirror. His face is his father's—a Nix face, not a Byrd or Loomis face. His mother uses Nix as shorthand for all things undesirable. He does something stupid, like gets arrested for robbing a convenience store: "That's your Nix blood coming through." If she just says Nix she does not have to say the other words. He locates a red bump that has cropped up in the crease by his nostril. "Little fucker." He tries squeezing it but can't get around it with the tips of his fingers. His eyes tear up and he sneezes.

The chair he selects for Peg is the last of an old dining room set that has been around since he was a kid, maybe longer. It is solid and sturdy, but before he carries it out he sits down in it and shimmies around and it doesn't so much as squeak. People of patience and skill used to take care making a small, mundane thing like a chair, he thinks. Who gives a shit, anymore, about a chair? He feels a slight, fleeting ache in some part of himself, in his chest perhaps, when he thinks of his own deficiency of craftsmanship, of handiwork. To no small degree, his failure at all forms of redneckery is why he went to college in the first place. College was, in effect, all he could do. He majored in history, with an emphasis on The American Civil War, and found some satisfaction in the praise of his professors. War, he thought, was a subject befitting a young man, a masculine topic, and his study of it, perhaps, compensated for his shortcomings. His favorite professor was Dr. Cyril Brown, a colorful southerner who told impossible stories of his Huck Finn boyhood and who liked to refer to The Civil War as "The War of Northern Aggression." A Kentucky Colonel, he had travelled with a circus when he was a teenager, had been a tightrope walker and a barker, and he had learned to barely miss young maidens with a throwing knife. Finally he'd tired of the circus and its shabby romanticism and decided to go to college. He didn't stop until he had earned a PhD.

Lucien took every class he taught, including Civil War through Letters, which had been his favorite. Dr. Brown had told Lucien on the last week of his last semester in college that he thought he was graduate school material and told Lucien he'd be glad to write him a letter of recommendation. Lucien thanked him and told him he would think about it, and Dr. Brown told him not to spend too much time thinking. What would Dr. Brown think, he wondered, of his present predicament?

Peg walks up the sidewalk carrying a twelve pack of Busch. As she draws closer, Lucien stands up to greet her.

"So where we working now?" He points at the empty chair, like a waiter, and takes the box of beer from her.

"I guess we'll have to wait and see." She sits in the good, sturdy chair.

Lucien cracks a beer and hands it to her.

Peg has a relieved, accomplished look about her, as if sitting down now and indulging in a drink or two, after going out and putting forth considerable effort, is a good thing, well earned. The day has warmed to all-out hot and she has unbuttoned the top two buttons on her thin blouse and strings of sweat-darkened blond hair stick to her glistening neck. She glances back at the house and takes a sip of her beer.

"Getting hot out." She puts the can of beer against her neck.

"I can get a cooler of ice for the beer."

"Wish you could leave here—come to my place."

"Me too. We can go inside if you want to."

"We can sit out here. Go get a cooler of ice, though, for the beer."

Lucien returns with a cooler full of ice-tray ice and a box fan plugged into an extension cord running from inside the house.

"Good thinking, college boy. Put it on high."

She closes her eyes and holds her hand out as if she is fighting hurricane force winds.

"Damn, never mind! Put it on medium."

Across the street, old man Preston has come out and is standing by his mailbox with a stack of mail in his hand. He takes a moment to look at them, sitting in the yard in mismatched chairs, in front of a box fan drinking cheap beer. Lucien sees him watching and becomes aware of the spectacle they must be to him.

Lucien holds up his beer and, loud enough for the old man to hear, says, "Cheers, Big Ears!" Looks at Peg.

Peg holds up hers. "Likewise, Piss Eyes!" And they bump their cans of beer.

Preston shakes his head and walks back inside.

"You never did tell me what you got that thing around your ankle for," says Peg, pointing her beer at it. She leans back in her chair, tilts it back on two legs.

"The law is making me."

"No shit, Sherlock."

"I shot a man."

She stares at Lucien with narrowed eyes.

"In Reno."

"Reno?"

"Yep. Just to watch him die."

She smirks.

"You're a goddamn Johnny Cash song."

"It's a coincidence."

She punches him in the arm.

"Fine, don't tell me, asshole."

"You'd think a whole lot less of me if you knew."

She puts her empty in the cooler and takes out a fresh one and pulls the tab on it.

"As long as you didn't do anything, you know, creepy." She sips her beer and looks at him sideways.

"What's considered creepy?"

"If you have to ask…"

"I didn't rape or molest anyone if that's what you mean."

"You sure about that? Hell, it's been a long time. Maybe you grew into some kind of weirdo. Fact is, I hardly know you now."

"It's just that it's kind of embarrassing. How it happened is stupid."

"You can do something stupid every once in a while. Just don't make a habit out of it."

Lucien drinks from his beer and sits quietly.

She readjusts the fan and moves her chair so that she is facing Lucien.

"Well, anyway, Justin told me you were back about three months ago."

"It wasn't like it was a secret."

"Some people didn't want me to know, especially after you got arrested."

"So you knew I got arrested?"

"Yeah, and I know why, too. I was just having fun with it—wanted to see if you'd tell me."

She sits up straight in the well-made chair and puts her finger to her chin.

"But let me make sure I got the chain of events right: graduate from college. Come back home. Meet up with some old friends and get drunk. Commit robbery with the biggest dumbass hick in town. Get put on house arrest. Mow the fucking lawn. Does that about cover it?"

"You forgot be reunited with the woman of my dreams."

"That's funny. Twenty-two years old, fresh out of college, and trying to impress a fucking hick like Casey Talbert. That don't make a damn bit of sense."

"I veered off track. It happens."

"You ain't lying."

"I think it's built into my DNA."

"What?"

"Ruin."

"You trying to make me puke?"

"What I mean is, I wanted to do it. It's almost like I had to do it." He stands up and walks a circle around his chair. "It gives me some dimension, don't you think?" He strikes a pose: part catalog model, part James Dean.

"I guess if you were looking to accentuate the moronic side of yourself—then, yeah."

"The gun was fake, by the way. He tricked me. How's that for moronic?"

Peg stands up and walks over to Lucien, gets close, so close their bodies touch at the
waist.

Lucien backs up. She moves toward him. She has a smirk on her face.

"Anybody can trick anybody. It don't mean nothing. You're better than he is."

Lucien backs up again and sips his beer.

"Says who?"

"Says me."

"All right, then. Let me ask you something. It's a good question to ask in a situation like this. Let's say you were broke down on the side of the road—in the middle of nowhere. It's dark, and the critters are closing in. Who would you want with you—Casey Talbert, or me? Who's the bigger dumbass in that situation, the dumb redneck who could fix your car, or the dumb, useless college boy?"

"I'd pick neither. Casey'd use it as an opportunity to get in my pants and you'd probably try talking the car back onto the road."

They laugh and Lucien moves forward, goes to embrace her. She moves into him and they stand like that for a moment. Lucien gives her a light kiss and she accepts it. When they break apart she looks down. The sidewalk is beneath them. "Loosh, look."

He jumps back into the grass, as if the sidewalk is on fire, as if it will help to be back in the grass, but it won't. He knows it won't.

"What do we do?"

"I don't know. Just wait for them to get here, I guess, and explain what happened."

"You think they're gonna care for an explanation?"

"Probably not a whole hell of a lot, no."

She puts out her hand.

"If they're gonna take you away whether you're a foot from your yard or a mile, might as well be a mile."

"Where would we go?"

"Wherever you want to."

Old man Preston is standing in his yard. He lights a cigarette, takes a drag and walks out to the edge of the road.

"Do me a favor!" he says. "When she gets back from wherever, tell that crazy-ass mother of yours to fire her lawn boy." He smiles, clearly pleased with himself for having thought of a comeback to their earlier taunt, even if his timing is a little off.

They run and walk for three miles until they make it to the flea market, which seems to them like a decent place to lay low until they figure out their next move. The flea market has a bar in the center of it that sells cheap lite beer in plastic glasses. A man sits on a stool in a corner nearby and strums a guitar and quietly sings what sounds like a George Jones tune. It feels like a good hiding place.

"I walked by your house almost every day for a month," says Peg, taking a drink from her cup of beer.

"I never saw you."

"I could only do it in the morning or late at night, until Dino's closed. Only took a week of afternoons after that."

"A week of afternoons," he says.

She rolls her eyes and takes a sip.

"They'll find me sooner or later—it'll be no more than a few days….You should go on home. You don't need to get yourself into any trouble."

"I'm not going anywhere. It's stupid, I know, but I'm not leaving you."

By the time they're done with their beers, they've thrown together a half-assed plan.

The Camellia Hotel lets rooms for ten dollars an hour, and between the two of them they have about fifty dollars. They get a room for two hours to regroup.

The room has a king-size bed and they both lay in it and stare at the ceiling.

"Air conditioning," whispers Peg in a tone of awe. "God bless the fucker invented air conditioning."

"You know what? I can't remember his name, but the dude that invented air conditioning was from Florida."

"Swamp-ass Florida: the birthplace of air conditioning. It's perfect."

They lay in silence for some time, both thinking about how they have ended up in this moment together. How it was both bad and good. How it will all end, and what will happen after it does.

"You have a lot of girls while you were away at college?"

"What kind of question is that?"

"A legitimate one."

"You have a lot of boys while I was away at college?"

"A few. I won't lie. I wasn't saving myself for anyone."

"I suppose I had a few too."

"Only a few?"

"Yes, only a few. Exactly a few—if a few means three."

"It doesn't matter to me. I was just curious."

At that she rolls over and straddles Lucien and they kiss and quietly undress each other, and it feels inevitable. They take it slow, as if they have a surplus of time, and when it is over, they fall asleep.

Peg wakes first. She uncovers Lucien and looks at his naked body, thin and boney but attractive to her. She looks at his torso and down from there and thinks how odd it looks, like something apart from him. She touches it softly and then quickly pulls her hand away. She takes time to look at the bracelet on his ankle. She touches it and wiggles it and, for the first time, in the relative dark of the hotel room, notices a very small blinking red light at the top of it, not much bigger than a pinprick. Lucien rouses and sits up.

"It got cold all the sudden."

"This little light here is blinking."

"Damn sure is. Kind of like a little tiny siren, ain't it?"

"It's sending them a signal. It's saying the same thing over and over again. Lucien is gone, Lucien is gone, Lucien is gone…"

"Something like that. Let's take a shower together."

They figure they can go directly to the police station, which would be the quiet, dignified approach, or they can just go back to the house, and call the police, and tell them to come and get him, that he'll be waiting. Peg almost convinces him to come to her place and call the police there, but Lucien decides against it, not wanting to cause a big to-do in her neighborhood. In the end they decide coffee would be nice first, so they walk from the Camellia to Denny's, only a few blocks away.

It's slow inside and they are immediately sat. Their waitress is a middle-aged woman with quick blue eyes and a nice but fading figure, a body that is becoming too tired for the strain of being beautiful.

"I really think you ought to go on home—leave me to this." Lucien sips his coffee and watches the line cook through the rectangular order window.

"I know you do. You're probably right. But I can't bring myself to leave you alone."

The cook strikes a bell with a long, skinny spatula and barks "Ord' up!"

The waitress walks up to their table and refills their coffee cups.

"I hate when they don't ask. You get your coffee just right and they come along and mess it up. It's a delicate balance."

"You always get hung up on such stupid shit?"

"Maybe. I been meaning to ask you. Why ain't you married to some big, strong country boy yet?"

"You mean someone like Casey Talbert?"

"Sure. Why not?"

"Because he's an idiot."

"I'll give you that. But there's plenty around here better than him. Plenty of good husband material."

"Maybe I'm not real big on tending to a doublewide all day and having big, dumb babies with some redneck sticks his head in cars for a living."

"It wouldn't be as bad as all that."

"Well, I figure, why add to all the white noise."

"If you don't like it here, if it's that bad, why haven't you left?"

"Guess I do kind of like it. In a weird way. Is that sick or something?"

"No. It ain't sick. I get it. I feel kind of the same way." He fixes up his diluted coffee.

"But you ever wonder if being ambivalent is the best you'll ever do?" The cook dings the bell and a skinny, young waitress hustles up and takes two plates out of the window and skitters off to a small table out of view.

"What about you? What are we gonna do about you?"

"We're just putting off the inevitable," says Lucien.

She pushes her coffee out into the middle of the table.

He pushes his too.

The police station is a mile walk from Denny's. They walk hand in hand along the cracked sidewalk, taking it slow. There's no reason to rush something like this. The sun is heading down now and it is not so hot out and a breeze blows lightly from the north and their moods lift some.

"This is good," says Lucien. "This is the right thing. I feel like I've come up against something and moved past it."

"Good?"

"Yeah. Good. I'll turn myself in, explain what happened, and they'll probably lock me up, but not for long. Bet I get thirty days, if that. Then when I get out, it'll all be over, and maybe we can pick up where we left off."

She squeezes his hand. "Not where we left off," she says. "You got to promise me. I don't care if it is in your DNA or whatever."

"I promise," he says. "I'm done with it. It's like I said: I just veered off track."

As they walk it gets cooler and a thunderhead appears on the horizon and flashes and grumbles and there comes a sound immediately behind them, on the road: gravel and road debris being crushed under a heavy weight. Lucien turns and sees a police car with tinted windows keeping pace with them.

He stops walking, pulls Peg into him and kisses her and then pushes her away.

"I guess this changes things a little bit," she says.

"Yeah," says Lucien. "Somewhat. But not substantially."

He walks along the white line toward the police car, his knees bent, arms out like wings. He starts wobbling back and forth. He takes a step back, a step forward. He starts moving his arms like a windmill, like he's losing his balance, like he's tightrope walking, and falls down to his side and lies there for a moment, arms and legs spread out, like he's dead. Peg laughs. The officer gets out of the car and walks over to Lucien and tells him to get his ass up, holds out his hand. He gently pushes Lucien against the car and Lucien puts his hands behind himself so that the officer can cuff them. With one hand the officer opens the backdoor of the cruiser and with the other he takes Lucien by the arm and guides him into the back seat. Peg looks into the car as it passes by her and she waves at Lucien. He can't wave but he has a smile on his face.

Death Comes for Noob Pierson

I've got it bad for Peg Vernon, head bartender at the Dew Drop Inn and champion of the Sahwoklee Catfish Festival Wet T-Shirt Contest, 1988 through 1991. Things that have nothing to do with Peg remind me of Peg. Just this morning, as I am shaking Navels out of a tree with a shiner pole, I watch Randall Ginny, two rows over, pelt Zeke Talbert up side the head with an orange, which gets me thinking about the time Peg caught Duke Richards in the back of the head with a full mug of beer, and how Duke didn't do nothing but curse and hop around, holding his head until the pain subsided, and then ordered a fresh beer on the promise that he'd behave himself for the rest of the night, and next thing I know I'm jolted back into the hot and muggy moment by one of Randall Ginny's overripe navel oranges, this one the size of a baby's head, breaking against my right shoulder blade.

"All the loose ones is shook off, fool!" He chucks another, but it misses me and breaks against the trunk of a tree. Randall Ginny, ignorant bastard extraordinaire, is my first cousin. He's been throwing shit at me for twenty years.

Picking fruit is okay for the Randall Ginnys of the world, but it's no job for a man with love on his mind. It's hard-ass illegal-Mexican type labor. Me, Randall and Zeke are the only non-Mexicans on our crew, and we're only there because Zeke Talbert's uncle, Jasper Talbert, runs the crew and pays us what he pays most of the senior-level Mexicans.

But I got other prospects. Got a black suit too. The manager of Foodex Supermarket # 032 said he was impressed with me, and I've got apps in at every other reputable place in town. It won't be long before I latch on to something good, and when I do, I'm going to ask Peg out on a bona fide date. I've been thinking of taking her to Hog Heaven, the best pit BBQ joint in Sahwoklee. They got a two-for-one special on margaritas from 4 till 7 every day, and the best baby back ribs I ever ate. Women love margaritas. Peg loves ribs.

But on this particular Friday afternoon, I'm right where I should be, cozily settled into my favorite centrally-located barstool at the Dew Drop Inn, talking to my future wife. The place is empty except for me and Peg, which is the way I like it. She starts pulling me a Natty and I tell her about my latest prospect: "Frank Moore, the top-head guy down at Foodex said he was impressed with my application. I got to get out of them groves, Peg. I'm determined. I've got plans for the future." Peg, being a good one for brevity, just says, "I reckon," and slides my beer over to me. Peg's hair is so blonde that when the light hits it just right it almost looks neon yellow. She sticks it up in the front with hair spray and you can tell by looking at it that it's the texture of insulation. Today she's wearing a black Skid Row tank top and stonewashed jeans with slyly located cuts and tears in them. I don't mind that she's a little older than me.

She's wiping down the bar, and I'm telling her about my five-year plan, when this dude walks in and sits down at the stool to my right and looks around the room like maybe he's being followed. But he's cool about it, like if he was being followed, it wouldn't really matter to him. He stares at me good and long, and nods, holds out his hand. He looks like he works at a law office or something. He's dressed in a dark blue suit and has a fresh haircut. He's just about perfect in every way. I'll admit it, he looks sharp. Peg makes eyeballs at him like he's some kind of hunk from heaven. I don't like the way things are shaping up.

"Name's Roger Firestone," he says.

I give his hand a tug.

"Name's Doug Crenshaw."

He orders a top-shelf double vodka on the rocks and while he waits for it he examines a red plastic cigarette lighter.

Peg slides his drink to him and he nods and puts a twenty on the bar.

I watch this guy and take an occasional swig of my beer. Once I get low, Peg fills me up again. I'm not comfortable with the way Peg is behaving towards this Firestone individual. She's got a newfound flirtatious way about her that makes me jittery. I try to subtly pull her attention away from Mr. Top-Shelf by jutting my elbow in the guy's direction and clearing my throat, but it's no use. This asshole's got her mesmerized. I wish I could do that, mesmerize. Peg was married once, by the way, to Lucien Nix, the King of All Mesmerizers. At one time or another, he'd mesmerized just about every eligible woman in Greater Cortez. But they was common law, actually, he and Peg. They never did officially tie the knot at the courthouse like most people, like I hope one day to do with Peg. Lucien was just too hot for "strange," as he called it, to officially get spliced up with just one girl. They've been split up for years now—five, I think—and she's up for re-mesmerizing. But I just can't seem to get the hang of it like this Firestone dude, like Lucien Nix.

Firestone swivels his barstool around and surveys his environs. He has his drink in one hand and the lighter in the other. He holds the lighter up in front of him and gives it a flick, moves it slowly from right to left across the room like it's a torch and he's in a cave. And I guess it is kind of like that inside the Dew Drop because it's only now that I notice there's one other person in here besides me, Peg, and this Firestone joker.

Noob Pierson is hunched over half a mug of beer at a table in the corner by the warped dart board that no one ever throws anything at but empty beer cans. Noob is old, but probably not as old as he looks. He has picked fruit his entire working life so he moves real slow and awkward and mechanical, like his body is made of dysfunctional machinery. It's painful to watch him walk. You think you can hear his joints creaking.

Roger stops moving his little torch once he sees Noob. Noob holds his arm up over his eyes like he's shading them from a bright light.

"The hell, son!?" Noob picks up his beer and turns his chair towards the corner. He looks like an angry troll.

Roger turns back to the bar, puts the lighter down and drains the rest of the vodka.

"I'll take another, please," he says.

Peg hustles over and gets to work on one.

Roger takes a cigarette out of a little golden box and lights it.

"That man in the corner there," says Firestone. "His name's Pierson."

"That's right," I say. "They call him Noob, Noob Pierson."

This Roger character puts his lips around the filter of the cigarette and gives it a long, elaborate suck. It's like he's making love to the damn thing. Peg slides him his vodka, and I'm pretty sure she winks at him. I'm not comfortable with this guy. He's cutting into my quality time with Peg.

"Want a smoke?" he says. "It's a real pleasure. To smoke." He looks at the cigarette like it's the best one anyone's ever had.

I tell him no thanks and he points the golden box at Peg. She takes one, and he lights it for her in a way I can only say is perverse. I'm feeling territorial as hell now. I can't recall ever having seen Peg smoke.

After a minute or two Noob pounds on the tabletop with his empty mug, the way he always does, and Peg gets him a fresh beer and walks it over to him.

Firestone quietly drinks his vodka. Everything this guy does he does like maybe he won't be able to do it again for a while. He closes his eyes when he drinks his vodka, swallows slowly like he's savoring every molecule of it.

"I don't think I ever seen you here," I say to him, hoping

to make him feel uncomfortable, hoping I can get him to leave.

"My first time," he says.

"You from Cortez?"

"Nope."

"Sahwoklee?"

"Nope."

"He aint much for conversating, is he, Peg?"

"Guess not," she says. She does her hand like a mouth, opens and closes it a few times, "But, then again, I can't stand a yapper." I swear they wink at each other in unison.

"Me neither," I say, and smile at Peg. She rolls her eyes, but I can't figure out why.

"You just leave a funeral or something?" says Peg.

"Hate funerals. Never been to one. I'll take one more," he says, holding up his glass.

"Must travel for work then…" I say.

"I do," he says. "A lot."

"I been looking for a more suitable form of employment myself," I add. "They's some prospects…." I glance at Peg and try out a wink on her and she sighs at me (a sigh of affection, no doubt). "But I wouldn't mind doing a little traveling."

He takes a slow sip of his fresh drink.

"Well, there's a real low turnover in my field," he says in a condescending tone that don't sit well with me, not in front of my lady like this.

"What field is that?" says Peg. That's it, I think. Interrogate this asshole, Peg.

"Basically," he says, and then pauses, "collections."

"I though they was always hiring in the collections field," I say.

"Like anything, it has its pros and cons," he says, kind of answering me, kind of ignoring me. "For instance," he continues, "what I collect, people don't always want to part with."

"Especially not vehicles," I say. "People on the TV shows don't ever let their vehicles go without a big fuss. So you're a repo man, then?"

Again, he don't answer me.

"Some think it's wrong, what I do," he says. "Some call it stealing."

"Well," I say, "as long as you can square yourself with it at the end of the day."

"Precisely." He points at me, which kind of startles me. "I don't take anything that I don't have a right to. Right Mr. Pierson?"

Noob does not respond. Peg stands behind the bar and dries her hands off with a little towel. She's looking agitated, now, completely *unmesmerized*, like she did that time before she threw the beer mug at Duke Richards.

"I don't trust the way you're beginning to talk, mister," says Peg. Peg don't put up with people who ain't straight talkers. After tending bar for all these years, she's developed a special kind of wisdom about these things. Firestone has veered off track. This ain't the way with Peg.

"You said you've never seen me here before," he says. "That's because I've never needed to come here until now.

Mr. Pierson over there has something it's my business to collect." He says this as if it explains everything.

I find it hard to believe that Noob has anything anyone would want. He's just a retired old drunk who lives in a singlewide behind the bar. He don't own nothing but a black & white TV and a rusty bicycle with two flat tires.

"You sure you don't have Noob mixed up with some other old-timer?" I say.

"I can't get mixed up."

"Noob's got shit," says Peg.

"That's right," I say. "Noob's got shit."

About this time Noob speaks up. "I got something," he says.

Firestone looks at me and smiles, and then looks over at Peg.

"See there? Mr. Pierson's got something. He ain't got much as you." Roger points at me with his cigarette. "Much as you." He points at Peg. "But he's still got something."

"Look," says Peg. "You better not start no shit in my bar." Peg keeps a sawed-off under the bar above the tap kegs. She moves closer to the edge of the bar.

Roger smiles and lights another smoke, takes a long, handsome toke of it.

"You've got to understand," he says, "Mr. Noob Pierson, here, is almost burnt up...on the inside." Roger exhales slowly. "He's nothing but embers." This strikes me as an unpleasant thing to say. I look over at Peg and she's welling up. She looks like she's about to burst open. I need to do something.

"Maybe it's time you took out of here," I say. "There's plenty a watering holes in Cortez. Elbow Room's just two miles up the road." I stand up, try looking intense and aggravated.

Firestone puts his lighter down, and before he can take a drink of his vodka, Peg's pointing the shotgun in his face.

He just sits there grinning.

"Boy's right. Time for you to take leave, mister." Her body has a little tremble to it. Her face is blotched red.

"She'll shoot you, my man," I say. I'm feeling anxious as hell, lit up, like my skin is burning. My girl Peg is on fire.

Roger stands up and extinguishes his cigarette. He puts his hands in the air.

"You've made me waste a cigarette," he says. "Let's go, Nelbert." He motions his hand toward Noob.

"You leave old Noob alone," says Peg. "He ain't got nothing nobody wants."

"That's right," I say. "Noob stays. You leave."

"If you need to, look at it this way," says Firestone. "I've got something Mr. Pierson wants."

By now old Noob is standing next to Firestone.

"I guess you want to get your face blowed off?" says Peg, looking so sexy standing there holding onto that gun. I have an urge to leap around, maybe onto the bar.

"I'm just doing my job," says Firestone, his hands still in the air. "I've got all the permission I need."

"It's all right," says Noob. "I'm a go with this feller. Put the gun down. I know this feller."

Peg slowly lowers the shotgun, looks hard at old Noob.

"As long as you know him, Noob" she says. "I guess it's all right." She's crying black eye makeup, but she looks solid, resolved, perfectly willing to shoot this man.

Roger Firestone walks towards the door. Noob is right behind him, moving more smoothly than ever. He no longer looks like you can hear his joints creaking. Peg and I watch until Firestone opens the door and the sunlight rushes in, and they both disappear into the light, and the place goes dark inside again.

"What the hell just happened!?" I say to Peg Vernon, professional bartender and woman of my dreams.

"Hell if I know."

"He wasn't no collections agent."

"No, he wasn't." She looks at the front door. "But he was a handsome devil, wasn't he?"

"Sure as shit was." I can't deny it. The guy is my hero, smoothness wise. I'm just glad he's gone.

The twenty dollar bill, the lighter and the golden cigarette box are still sitting on the bar. I take a cigarette out of the box and light it and hand it to Peg. She takes it with a shaky hand. She looks kind of crazy now with black streaks down both cheeks, still holding onto the shotgun with one hand. She takes a drag of the cigarette and when she exhales it's like all the tension and anxiety inside of her go out with the smoke. She looks insane as hell to me, the future Mrs. Crenshaw, and I like it.

The Cornish Cross

She's queen of the hill. She barely moves except for a little jerk of her tiny dumb head, a balk in one direction and another, as if at a loss on which way to go, oblivious to his presence. Finally he pulls the trigger, and she drops to one side and flaps and tosses, making a ragged circle as she kicks and flutters. Liam whinnies and sidesteps. Tadpole sets down the rifle, walks over and picks her up by the feet and examines her. He notices me sitting in the bus, looking out the window at him.

"What the hell you looking at?" I shoot him the bird, spit half a peanut hull toward him. I like messing with him. He's smarter than the rest of us and can knock the ass end off a tick with that rifle. I'll clean the chicken and cook it for him.

He sits down on a busted cinderblock for a while, stares at the dead bird laid out in the dirt in front of him. He pulls a sandspur off his ankle and flicks it. Sandspurs are all over the ground this time of year. You got to watch your step.

I look up the empty road. I begged them to stay. It's best when we all stay together, without any interruptions. But now that they're gone, I don't want them to come back.

The dry autumn air feels light and cool when it pushes through the window, makes me think of Michigan and how we did not go and how cold we'd be right now if we had. I hate picking apples. I hate the cold. There was a boy up there named Kevin Merchant whose daddy owned an orchard. He was tall and had thick blond hair. Handsome and clean, he walked around like a rooster, followed his daddy everywhere.

Tadpole needs to put a shirt on. He's liable to catch cold.

I'm still sitting in my seat. It's the only part of this bus that don't look like pure shit. I'm watching a Tom and Jerry cartoon on my little black-and-white TV I got perched on top of a small citrus crate wedged into the corner behind the seat in front of mine. Cartoons don't look that great without color, but it's better than nothing. I've done my best to make this small pocket of space mine. I got my stuffed animals crammed in around me on the seat, and I took and wrote ENID across the back of the seat in front of mine with a black marker. I like my surroundings to look nice. I take care of my things and myself. My body is always clean. I do my hair up nice. Right now it is in a tight French braid, which is a hard thing to do to your own hair. Boys don't give a shit, don't notice. Except that boy Kevin in Michigan noticed. He told me my hair was pretty. He got my attention that way.

Herschel's in the back of the bus hunched over Sarah, giving her hell. She likes it. Makes me sick. She cusses things at him, calls him names. Herschel tells her to shut up. I can't take it no more, so I go outside.

"What you gonna do with her now that you shot her? Don't nobody *shoot* a chicken, by the way." I stretch the tired out of my body with a shiver. I've just been sitting in that bus all day. Feels good to be outside of it.

"What's it to you?"

"Pa beat your ass for killing one of Baird's chickens."

"He ain't here. And I ain't fulled up on boiled peanuts like some people."

"I won't clean it." I'm only teasing him.

"The hell you won't."

I sit down on the bottom bus step. I roll up the leg of my jeans and rub at a raspberry on my shin that I got when I scraped it up against a cinderblock barricade I climbed to get to the phosphate mine I bathe and wash my clothes in. We're a collection of sore spots, the Baggott children, forever bruised and scabbed and sprained and twisted—if not from roughhousing and horseplay then from Pa, who swears he'd never lay a hand on any of his precious children and never remembers when he does. At least he don't have roaming hands. I'll take a fist over a roaming hand any day of the week.

"Wring her neck," I say.

"I don't think you do that if you shot it," says Tadpole. He walks over next to her. He holds the chicken up close to his face. He flicks at the red Mohawk of flesh on her head.

"Do it regardless," I say.

Tadpole slowly takes hold of her soft, fine-feathered neck, whips her full circle and drops her in the dirt. Her feet dance and kick up a few little clouds of dust.

"That'll do," I say, standing close to Tadpole now. "You wrung the remnants of life out of her."

"She was mostly already dead," he says, with a bob of his head.

By now Sarah is standing outside by the bus.

"Better not be one of Daddy's Crosses," she says.

"This here's a stray," says Tadpole. He holds it behind his back, as if someone is trying to grab it from him. "It's got nothing to do with you."

"It ain't like it's a goddamn pussycat, little boy," says Sarah. She walks up next to Tadpole and me. "It's poaching, or something like that. Anyway, it's stealing, for sure."

"You won't say a goddamn word about it, will ya?" says Herschel, stepping out of the bus, wearing nothing but faded blue jeans, unbuttoned at the top. Sometimes he makes me sick.

"Can't just go around shooting people's livestock. They'll haul you to jail for that," says Sarah. "Y'all some sorry white folks, I tell ya."

Sarah is Baird's only child. She is fifteen, two years younger than Herschel. Her father owns the crescent of pasture and farmland, roughly 800 acres, that nearly encircles the five acres we live on. She is often barefoot, by choice, and wears pretty, flowing dresses, and rides Liam, the ornery paint, just about everywhere. She's bright and devious and frightening to boys her own age. I'm not jealous of her. If I was Herschel, being seventeen years old, I would be gone by now. Why does he stay here? Why live in a shitty old school bus if you don't have to? He *is* sorry. Me and Tadpole are not, but he is. It must be Sarah that keeps him here. He's sweet on her, and not just for what they do in the back of the bus and out in the woods. I bet he loves her, not that he'd own up to it, or even say it like that if he did, or even understand that that's what it was.

"Get on out of here, then," says Herschel. He takes out his pecker and shakes it at her. Tadpole laughs.

"Not a problem," says Sarah. "I shouldn't be seen in the company of larcenists, anyhow." She walks over to Liam, unhitches him, mounts him, and takes off down the trail, through the woods, toward home.

Tadpole pokes a finger at the chicken carcass and juice spurts and hisses into the flames. Twilight is coming on, and it is quite cool out for early fall, but not as cool as it is in Michigan, which is where we usually are this time of year; Michigan in early fall, for apple picking, then back down to Florida in late fall and winter for the citrus harvest.

"Get your dirty meatbeaters off of it. It ain't ready yet," I say. I walk over next to him and sit down on a long twisted oak log by the bonfire. I throw him a gray sweatshirt, and he puts it on. Herschel thinks I'm always babying him. But I'm not. I'm just taking care of him. It's a normal thing to do. Even animals take care of their family members, for a while at least. Sometimes people don't even behave as good as animals do. After a long day of picking apples, when a handsome boy tells you you got pretty hair and asks you to go for a walk with him, you go.

I take Tadpole around the waist and sit him on my knee and give his burr-head a muss. He is small for an eight-year-old. His head is shaved because he had lice on it. Thinking about lice makes my head itch.

"You ain't scared of no chicken, are you?" I say.

"Who the hell's scared of a chicken?" he says.

I hear a dry rustle of branches from the woods, and Tadpole jumps off my knee and picks a sword-size stick up off the ground. He holds it up and then swishes it around a few times, trying it out, feeling the heft of it. Off in the distance, in the eastern woods, a bobcat tears loose a scream. Tadpole drops the stick and runs back over to the log and sits down next to me. He knows what it is, but the lady-cry of one always startles him. Startles me too, sometimes, when I'm not expecting it, conjures up images of ugly things I got no name for but know something of. I told that Kevin boy, no barns. I won't go in no barn with you, I said. He smiled and pointed toward the orchard, and I went with him. He had broad shoulders and nice clean work boots on, and his blue jeans were tight, and he had a way about him. He wasn't nothing like us, like Herschel. Didn't lumber around, bent a little, from being hunched over things most his life. He'd gone to college some, too. But he didn't like it. It was dusk, and once you got into that orchard, it was dark.

I get up and take the chicken by the leg and whip it around on the grate, causing a commotion of hisses in the fire below it.

About then Herschel comes walking out from the darkening edge of the woods. He walks slowly around the fire and sits down on a bench seat come out of a junked pickup-truck.He spits in the fire.

"Where you been?" I say.

"Smells pretty good," he says.

"You ain't had nothing to do with it," I say.

"Uppity bitch," he says.

"Why don't you go fuck yourself?" I say.

He gets up and walks around the fire and sits next to Tadpole. I stay next to the fire, minding the chicken.

"Fixing to be done," I say, staring into the fire.

He picks up Tadpole and slings him over his shoulder and starts jogging around the fire. "Sack a taters! Sack a taters!"

"Turn me loose!" says Tadpole. He scissor-kicks his legs against Herschel's back and he tosses him down in the dirt at his feet. Tadpole curls up, holding his stomach, gasping for breath.

"Knocked the breath out of him, asshole," I say. I walk over to give Tadpole a hand up, and Herschel puts a foot against my head as I squat toward my little brother, causing me to fall back. The top of my head lands on the edge of the fire. I hear my hair sizzle, and I scream. Tadpole screams, too. Herschel grabs the chicken off the grate and hurls it into the woods. It hits some branches and then thuds to the ground.

"What you gonna eat now?" he shouts, and almost in answer, Liam comes trotting slowly out of the woods. He is still saddled, but no one is riding him.

Herschel walks closer, and Liam blows; his ears are pricked forward, and his eyes are wide and bright.

Tadpole and I are in the bus now. I have a wet towel on my head.

The horse snorts. A bobcat moans again off in the woods. It sounds close. It makes Tadpole shiver. Herschel takes a slow step toward the horse and caresses his neck. "It's all right, boy." Liam snorts and digs a hoof into the ground. Herschel makes a kissing sound and keeps petting his neck. Once the horse seems calm, he yells to me to bring him a flashlight.

"Liam's out here!" he says

Back by the fire I hand Herschel the flashlight, and he shines it on Liam as the horse patiently stands there. My brother is cruel, like Pa. Why hasn't he left? Maybe he doesn't want to leave Sarah. I believe he loves her. My hair is ruined.

Kevin wanted to walk behind me. I didn't say nothing. I got a strange feeling and stopped, and he pushed me in my back and said, walk, and I walked.

"Probably just got loose of the stable somehow," I say.

"Why's he still wearing the saddle, then?" says Tadpole.

Me and Herschel look at Tadpole, smart little shit.

I take the wet towel off my head and press on the tender spots with the palm of my hand. "I can't go nowhere like this." My French braid is still in, but I got bald spots. I feel the urge to cry but force it back down past my throat and put the towel back on my head. No crying in front of Herschel. No crying in front of anyone.

"We'll need to get you a wig," says Tadpole. He walks over to me and puts his hand on my back.

"Should I ride him home?" says Herschel.

"Fuck if I care what you do with your girlfriend's horse."

"Fuck if I care too," says Tadpole.

"Be bad Ma and Pa find it here. Can't imagine what they'd want to do with it."

"Hell," I say, "might be fun to watch you try and ride it." I sit down on the log. Tadpole puts a plastic grocery bag in the fire, and we watch it shrivel into nothing.

"Go on," I say. "Mount him."

"Maybe I ought to lead him along. He looks fine, but he's spooked."

"Bet it's that bobcat out there that scared him," says Tadpole, quickly glancing around.

"Suit yourself. Take you a lot longer that way."

"I know." He grabs hold of the reins and gives a tug and gets Liam to turn back toward the trail in the woods that leads to the Baird house. The horse seems eager to go.

"You wait up for me?"

I just stare at him. Tadpole pulls his sword out of the fire. The tip of it glows a deep, mean orange. He turns and looks at Herschel and holds the stick so that the tip points at him

"Sorry about your head. I was just roughhousing. I didn't mean for you to catch fire."

It was cold and dark in that apple orchard. I'm not stupid, I went for it. I bolted, but that boy was fast, and he took hold of me by my hair—my long, beautiful hair—and he slung me down in front of him, and he got on top of me. He smiled the way he done when he told me my hair was nice, but it looked different now. It was cold and dark in that apple orchard. He put his knees on my arms. He slowly unbuttoned my shirt and put a hand on my breast. His hand was soft, like a child's.

"What about the chicken?" says Tadpole. "That was just meanness."

"Yeah," I say. "What about the goddamn chicken?"

"I'll see if I can bring something back with me."

"I'll wait up till I get tired—hour, hour and a half. But then I'm going to bed."

When Herschel arrives back at the camp I am sitting by the fire with a ratty blanket wrapped around me. Tadpole is curled up under the end of my blanket in the dirt by my feet, asleep, like a dog. The fire crackles and spits and puts a devilish orange hue on everything around us.

"Bout time," I say softly once I notice Herschel standing on the other side of the fire. I do not want to wake Tadpole.

Tadpole stirs anyway and gets up and sits on the log with me. I bring him into the blanket. He shivers. "You bring anything to eat?"

"No. I didn't."

"Ma and Pa are in the bus," I say, nodding toward the hulk of fading yellow paint and gray Bondo. Our broke-down home. "Passed out. They was drunk as skunks."

"Sarah's dead. Found her on the trail bringing Liam back."

Tadpole gets up and runs into the bus.

"She was twisted up. Figure Liam got spooked and throwed her."

"What did you do with her?" I say, and can't help thinking, *dumb bitch*, even though I don't really mean it.

He tells me about coming across her on the trail, about how she looked, how her body was twisted across the trail in the attitude of a swimmer arrested in mid-stroke. He tells me everything.

"Then I saddled her to Liam and walked her home and left her there with Baird."

"Jesus, what did he do?"

"Not much. Sent me off." He kicks at the ground. "None of this would've happened we'd a gone to Michigan, like we was supposed to."

"Yeah," I say, "it wouldn't've. But something would've." And I think of that boy Kevin. I think of the walk back to our camp after being in the orchard with him. How Pa was already drunk. And I think of the way Pa looked at me and my cold face that wanted to cry but wouldn't. And how he looked at that no good boy and saw the smirking heat of violence in his face. And how he smirked back and nodded, and how that boy said, good night, just as natural as could be.

I think about how I knew that night that I was alone.

After a time lights come shining up into the camp. We turn and see a pickup coming up the dirt road. It comes to a stop in front of the bus, and we can tell that it's Baird's.

He does not immediately get out of the truck. He lets the headlights shine and sits there in the cab for a short while.

We stand by the fire and wait.

The driver's side door creaks open, and Baird puts a foot out and then the other, and when he shuts the truck door we can see by silhouette that he has the butt of a gun tucked under his arm. He walks slowly forward, gets to the fire and stares into it. We watch him.

"Sorry for your loss, Mr. Baird," I finally say, not sure I should have said anything at all.

He spits in the fire and reaches into his pocket and pulls out two shells and jostles them in the palm of his hand for a moment, like dice, and then busies himself with loading them into the gun.

"Sorry," he says. "You are sorry, young lady. Just a family of lazy-ass goddamn bus dwelling lowlifes."

Neither Herschel nor I speak. I glance up at the bus and see a low glow of light in a window at the far end. The quiet is painful.

Baird tucks the gun back under his arm and sighs and looks over at his truck. "We took and rode over." He turns and smiles sickly at us. The fire casts some light on his face, distorted by anguish.

"You got her in the truck there with you?" I say, gathering up the blanket and pulling it tighter around my body.

He does not respond.

"I hope you don't think none of us had nothing to do with it, sir," says Herschel, his voice weak. "I just found her is all." He points at the trailhead. "Liam come up out of there—right there—and then I took—"

"I know you was carrying on with her, boy," says Baird. "That's the onliest thing worth considering." He takes a couple steps back and slowly raises the barrel of the gun. He jerks his head to the right. "Step away from your brother, there, girl. Less you want buckshot blowed all over you."

I do not move.

"Go on, now. Get clear of there." He's just about crying now. I want to feel sad for him, but I don't.

"You gonna have to shoot both of us," I say, and mean it, and feel it. I quickly reckon I'm ready for whatever might happen. I don't care for Herschel. He could die, and I wouldn't feel too much, one way or another, but I feel this is right. If I'm alone, he is alone, and I feel sorry for him for only that reason. There's no pain or fear worse than loneliness, and fear of pain has long been pounded out of me. Nor am I frightened by the prospect of leaving this world, if it comes to that. What would I be leaving? What would I become? If there is Heaven, it will be so much better than this. Hell would just be more of the same. Neither? If there is just *nothing*? Nothing would be peace. Whatever there is or ain't, I figure I have it covered. My only worry is for Tadpole, who, in my absence, will have no one to look after him. But he is smart, and he will make do, if it comes to it.

"That suits me just fine," says Baird. He pumps the gun's forearm and braces himself, and there comes a shot, followed by a high-pitched report, which is not the loud clap of a shotgun blast, but the sound of the twenty-two Tadpole has stuck through a back window of the bus. What follows is a dense, engulfing quiet, in which Baird's body hangs, like a marionette's, not falling, arrested, but eventually angling back, stiffly, almost like a plank of lumber, a gray wall of dust leaping up from the ground around him, drifting there in the firelit night, slowly, slowly curling back into itself, and fading finally into the crisp, gentle breeze of autumn.

Love in Sahwoklee

If there is such a thing as a beginning, this is it: a typical Friday evening and we were playing pool at the Golden Q, and in she walked, like she knew we'd be there, looking like she'd just crawled out of an abandoned library basement. There was a gnomishness about her, like maybe she'd been exposed to something toxic as a child. Her hair, the color of dead leaves, looked brittle, like if you touched it or blew on it the wind would carry it away. The other women in the place were your typical pool-hall types, rough beauties who had done too much of all the wrong things and were attractive until you got up close and all the hurt came into focus. They had to work too hard for their provisional good looks. Of course, me and Lance were no different. We were no one's dreamboats, no one's white-horse riders.

She sat down at the bar and ordered a drink, swiveled around and watched us play pool. Once I got a better look at her I realized she was familiar.

"I think I know who that is," I whispered to Lance.

"No shit?" he said. "Maybe you could introduce us. I like the way she looks."

I was in need of refreshment so I walked up to the bar and stood next to her and ordered a beer. She didn't budge.

"Your name Jasmine?"

She squinted at me, like she was trying to read a tiny font. "Yep. Your name Barry?"

I did not yet have a reason to lie to her, so I told her it was.

"I remember you," she said.

"Yep," I said. "You look a little different."

She told me I did too, but she was wrong, because I looked essentially the same as I did in high school. I asked her where she'd been.

"College and grad school, etc." I'd never heard anyone say "etcetera" before. She looked bored with the subject matter.

"For ten damn years?"

"Yep."

"That's a lot of etcetera. Should I be calling you Dr. Jasmine Dingle, then?"

Again, just a yep.

"What the hell you doing back in Cortez? Shouldn't you have some fancy job?"

"Maybe I do."

"Don't look like you do."

"I don't," she said. "I'm an adjunct. Teach composition at Sahwoklee Junior College. Just started this week. Staying at my parents' for now."

"What you teaching them the composition of?"

"Funny," she said.

About then Lance waved me over. He had an agitated look on his face.

"You trying to horn in on my action?"

Hell, no!" I said. "She looks like a reanimated corpse. Smells like old books. I don't want nothing to do with her."

I had my eye on Belle Crawford, actually, who was playing pool at a table on the other side of the place. Belle was composed of perfectly located hills and dales, God's Country, always in tight jeans and skimpy halter-deals.

"Well, I'm gunning for that gal right there," said Lance, "whether you introduce me or not. I like the look of her. She seems worldly."

Truthfully, this was not a huge surprise. In the five years we'd been friends, Lance had never expressed an appreciable interest in any of Cortez's beauties. (I even thought at one point that maybe he was homosexual, which would not have bothered me.) Also, in hindsight, it seems to me now that he could be found watching Shelley Duvall and Sissy Spacek films at a higher frequency than what you could call random or coincidental.

"If you say so," I said. "I'll introduce you to her."

Worst goddamn decision I ever made.

After they'd been going together for a few weeks, I started to get the impression that things were getting serious. Lance got to where he had her over to his trailer three or four nights a week. He and I hung out together less and less. I decided that I'd need to have a word alone with Jasmine Dingle, Ph.D. It was my feeling that some parameters needed to be set.

I was at this place called The Nine Ball, *sans* Lance, one Saturday night when the opportunity presented itself. Belle

Crawford, my girlfriend now, was with me. In walked Jasmine. I waved her over and she kind of went limp with disappointment and scuttled across the room like a dismounted scarecrow.

Belle said, "Hi, Jasmine," real pleasant and fake-genuine, like she was happy to see her, even though she wasn't, and Jasmine scoffed at her and said in a sarcastic tone, "Hi, Belle," spitting out the *B* in Belle like it had a bad taste to it.

She sat on a barstool next to the wall and drank lite beer while we played pool. Eventually Belle had to leave and I bought Jasmine a fresh beer and mounted the stool next to her.

"Where'd your girlfriend run off to?"

"She's gonna be a bridesmaid this weekend."

That's delightful," she said, but in a way that made you feel like she meant the opposite.

"You and Lance seem to be doing real good," I said.

She did not respond.

"I guess things are pretty serious between you two."

Again, nothing.

My approach was off. I sat quiet for a while.

"You know what?" she said, finally, startling me.

"What's that?" I said.

"I remember you quite well from high school." She took a sip of her beer. "Well, the bit of high school you made it through, anyway."

That seemed liked an ugly thing to say, and I told her so.

"I'm sorry," she said. "Sometimes things just come out that way. I can't always help it."

I thought of the way she'd said *Belle*, spitting out the *B.*

"I remember you too," I said, took a drink. "I remember you running home from school. Always running." (My parents' home was, and still is, on the same street as Cortez Senior High.

She smiled. "I liked running. It's something I think I could have been—a runner. I bet I was fast."

I smiled back. "I bet you was too," I said.

"I'm a little embarrassed to say it," she said, "but I had a small crush on you back then." She quickly took a sip of her beer, so she could hide behind the mug.

Good god! I thought. We're having a moment here. I struggled for a response.

"Well," I said, "I wish you'd have told me that way back then."

"Really?" She perked up, and I caught a rare glimpse of her pretty little running-and-smiling face. "Why is that?"

"That way I could have got to you before you went off to college and got all uglied up."

Her little rag doll face tensed up, and she hurled the contents of her beer mug at me, hopped off the stool and skittered out of there. I finished my beer in damp contemplation of my profound stupidity.

I shouldn't have said it. I should have told her I'd thought she was cute, too, back then, because that was the truth. But it just came out backwards. It was the truth on top of the other truth, crossways—the same truth, but in reverse.

If I had just dug a little deeper everything that followed wouldn't have happened. If I had had any control over things this incident ended it and put me on a bad course with Jasmine, and I stayed on it. I'd put myself there, but she did little things here and there, like small corrective hand movements on a steering wheel, to keep me rutted, smart gal that she was, with her college degrees and all that. I'm pretty sure she'd decided that from that moment on she was gonna save things up and use them against me once she saw the opportunity. And she did. She sure as shit did.

For obvious reasons, Jasmine didn't want me to be the best man at the wedding. Her brother, Roger, ended up pulling duty. Lance didn't even like Roger, who's a real asshole, one of them mobile phone-wielding computer geeks. I could tell it bothered Lance that I wasn't gonna be his best man, but there wasn't nothing he could do about it. He told me he was sorry and I ended up coordinating his bachelor party instead.

I didn't really have a whole lot planned. I rented out Golden Q for the night and had Wing Ding cater the party. I almost forwent the traditional stripper thing, because I didn't figure they had Lance's type of woman as strippers, but it turned out they did. I called up Cortesian Courtesans, the most venerable stripper service in the greater Cortez area.

"Look here," I said. "I'm looking to hire a stripper for my buddy's bachelor party, and I have a special request."

The guy on the phone started telling me about all these real beauties they got, boom and bang and bing and oh baby, and all that kind of junk, but I cut him off.

"No," I said. "That work. This is different." I paused. Let's put it this way," I said. "If you've got her, send me over Hugh Heffner's worst nightmare." It was the most accurate way I could think to describe her.

There was silence, some throat clearing. I thought maybe he was going to hang up. But he didn't.

"I know just what you mean," he said. "I've got just the girl, a cross between, say, a stenographer and a Denny's waitress."

"You mean you got a gal like that that works there?"

"Of course, all shapes and sizes. All women are beautiful in some way. Beauty is a very subjective thing," he said in a professorial tone. You could tell he meant what he said.

We played pool and darts and drank and ate wings and listened to music and when the stripper came she was perfect. She was dead on what I'd hoped for for Lance. She even sort of looked like Jasmine. She came in dressed as Ms. Tidy, the Health Inspector, and had a couple of the guys fooled. She put down her briefcase on the bar and pulled out a little boom box and turned on some Paula Abdul song or something and danced over to Lance and pushed him into a chair and rubbed herself, what little there was of her, all over him and he loved every damn second of it.

They got married at the Sahwoklee County Courthouse, just the two of them, and her brother Roger, as best man, which is hard to picture in any kind of happy way. I wasn't there, but it seems to me like it must have been the most depressing wedding in all of human history. Or, at least, Sahwoklee County history.

I met them at the Nine Ball afterwards and we played some pool and drank a few pitchers of beer. By now I was broke up with Belle. She was pretty, but she was dumb as an empty beer can. I'd got bone tired of listening to her go on and on about Dr. Phil and her teacup poodle, Trixie, whose nails she kept painted lipstick red and whose microscopic head was permanently garnished with a pink bow. Once our lovemaking had achieved a routine sameness there was nothing there anymore. We'd do the deed and then sit around smirking at each other while Trixie growled gutturally at me.

That night Roger tried hooking me up with some pencil-pushing gal from his work. Her name was Nancy Swanson, but she wanted you to call her "Nan." She was tall and shaped like a Bartlett pear. She had a thing for wearing corduroy pants and carried a chain wallet. I asked Roger if he was sure she wasn't a lesbo and he assured me she wasn't, but I wasn't convinced. He was the type of guy who'd set up something like that just to watch it go down. She was nice, but I wasn't interested in pear-shaped dykes. I drove her home that night, but I did not get out of the car, and she seemed okay with that.

They'd been married for a little over two years when it happened. It had been a rare good night for the three of us. I'd come over to their trailer that afternoon after work, and she was in a good mood because she'd found out that she was being considered for a tenure-track position at the community college, which would mean job security, and, according to her, was a sure thing, because she was that damn good. Plus she was excited about the prospect of teaching *real* classes, not just comp and freshman- and sophomore-level literature courses. So we had a little celebration type thing happening. All the annoyance and anger we'd caused each other in the past was pushed aside for the night, as a matter of convenience, so that we could enjoy her inevitable success. We cooked out on their back deck and drank some lite beers and laughed and talked about things and Jasmine, it seemed, was really not minding my company. If I played my cards right and didn't do anything major to piss her off many nights like this one lay before us. I saw a future where we were all friends for years to come, one where we spent lots of good, happy times together. Maybe I'd even find me a woman to marry and we'd be two married couples doing shit and growing old together. But the general mood of the evening changed pretty quick.

We're done eating, have cleaned up, and are sitting on their back porch drinking and enjoying the cool evening and Lance turns to me and has a look on his face like he used to when we were just two free-flying bachelors and he says, "Let's go hunting?" He gives me a wink.

I look over at Jasmine, and her little scrunched up body stiffens and she looks at me like she's back to hating me.

"You sure that's a good idea, buddy?" I say.

"Hell, yes! It's been forever, ain't it?"

She gets up and walks over next to Lance. "I don't like that idea," she says, her bony little arms crossed over her chest.

"Yeah," I say, "might not be the best night for it."

"Bullshit," he says. "Bullshit to both of you." He takes a sip of his beer and fidgets in his seat, says something under his breath about *two goddamn years.*

"Listen to your friend, Lance," she says.

"Fuck it," he says. "Just forget it."

"Don't get mad. Don't ruin a good night," she says. "This was a good night."

"I ain't mad," he says.

Jasmine walks off the deck and goes inside.

"Guess I better be going," I say, and Lance ignores me.

I go in and tell Jasmine goodbye. I tell her that I've had a nice time and have really enjoyed her company, which I had. I actually had. I wasn't lying. She forces a smile and says, "I had a pretty good night too." She thanks me for discouraging Lance from going out. "Oh, of course," I say. And I feel like things are special, like I might be able to level with her, so I go for it.

"Look," I say. "I want to tell you something."

But she puts a hand up and says, "Stop. Stop right there. Don't get carried away," she says. "You're still number one on my shit list." She sticks up her index finger and looks at it, then at me. "Number fucking one."

"Well, how can I get off that list?" I say.

"I don't know," she says. "You really hurt my feelings. What you said." She tightens the knot of her arms across her narrow chest and then she lets them fall to her side.

I start to say something, something like sorry, but she says, "Just go, please," so I go.

I am not ready to go home, so I stop by the Jiffy for a twelve pack of Busch and decide to head on out to our hunting spot by myself. It's really more of a drinking spot. It's just a clearing out in the middle of some acreage my uncle Jessup owns. It's drinking with guns, what we did out there, not hunting. Occasionally we'd fire at some rustling in the woods. But that's about it. It's not even, strictly speaking, legal. But Jessup didn't care so there wasn't much the authorities could do about it.

I'm out there, sitting on the tailgate of my truck, having a beer, my thirty-thirty propped up next to me and, for a time, I reckon the disruption Jasmine Jasper (née Dingle) has caused to my life, and it occurs to me that that's what I am to her, as well. We are in each other's way. One cannot exist unimpeded without the other. It is an untenable situation. Even if we liked each other, things would be basically the same. One of us would have to go. Three don't work. After my second beer, I start feeling tired. I lie back in the bed of the truck and look up at the tops of the pine trees and the stars beyond them. It's getting kind of chilly, so I grab an old flannel and put it on. In a few minutes I'm out. I don't know how long I'm asleep, but I wake up to some rustling in the distance. I grab the gun and sit still on the tailgate of the truck. I hear the rustling, getting louder and closer. I pick up the rifle and hold it close to my chest. It's quiet for a moment, then it ain't, and I jump off the tailgate and point the rifle in the direction of the sound and fire and everything stops.

Everything stops.

I remember there's a flashlight in the cab of my truck. I get it and walk with the gun and the light in the direction the sound had come from. I start getting a sick feeling as I walk. I get about six feet into the woods and goddamn. I see the toe-box of a work boot. I puke right there, on the spot. I drop the gun and the light and fall down on the ground. The flashlight shines up, slantways, into the tall pines. Mockingbirds start to chatter in the woods around me. It's early morning now, and everything is damp from the dew. I know he's dead, even though I ain't seen nothing but a foot.

Finally I get off the ground and pick up the flashlight and work up the courage to shine it. He's got a hole in his forehead. Right goddamn in the center of his forehead. An impossibly perfect shot. But that ain't it, either. When I go to pick him up, the top of his body feels pinned to the ground. I grab his shoulder and pull him into a sitting position and I see there's a sharp tree stump about a foot long and about six inches around, straight through his back, next to his shoulder blade. There's a case of beer about six feet away, with its corner lodged into the dirt, positioned like a diamond coming up out of the ground.

I drag him up to the bed of my truck and, with the aid of a makeshift pully system I made with a spool of nylon rope fed through the driver-side window, manage to lay him in.

I ain't gonna lie. I sat there and drank a beer. I drank a beer and looked him over and thought about what to do, and I thought about everything that had happened leading up to that moment. How strange it felt to be stuck in a moment; to look back and see a kind of choreography of actions that lead up to the time you're in and see the seeming inevitability of it. Was this always going to happen? Had time just been waiting for me to catch up—to do this— so that we could carry on?

I thought about burying him and taking off. Just disappearing. I had some time. I could have got a good piece up the road before anyone found any reason to start looking into things. I could have got clear to West Texas, probably. Clear to Virginia. Clear to Key West. But I didn't. I felt like I had to do right by my buddy Lance. So I hopped in my truck and drove the dead son of a bitch to the hospital. At the hospital, I told them everything. I even told them about Jasmine and how cruel I'd been to her. I told the truth like a confession, and telling the truth landed me here, and the song of these last ten years has played on without my hearing a single note.

The Cone of Possibility

Will stood at the end of the driveway—looked up and down the quiet street. There was an uncommon stillness in the air—a deep hush that a light breeze seemed to push toward him from the woods just south of the trailer park in which he lived—a collective, primordial pause that Will felt and could almost see, like a fog.

"I hope it comes," he said. With his eyes closed he breathed in the foreboding air.

"Hope what comes?" It was Russ, a ten-year-old boy who lived in the trailer directly behind Will's.

"Damn, Russ. Can't be ambushing people like that."

"Why ain't you at work?" Russ was barefoot and wore blue jeans his legs had long outgrown. He wore a pin-striped t-shirt, short enough to show a sliver of his flat white stomach. Russ wondered why he was not in school but didn't ask.

"I'm feeling poorly," Will said, pretending to be ticked off. He noticed Russ scratching his sweaty arms while standing there next to him.

"What you digging at yourself for?"

"Is there a hurricane coming?" Russ put his arms straight to his sides and tried hard not to scratch at them. "I heard a hurricane's coming."

"Maybe. News said it might be here early tomorrow morning. Let me see your arm."

Russ lifted his left arm up to Will's face. Will pulled it closer and examined it, rotating it back and forth, so he could see Russ's whole forearm. A few quarter-sized red areas tattooed each arm, as well as a few S-shaped bumpy areas scabbed up from Russ scratching at them.

"Itches like hell," said Russ.

"You got scabies."

"Scabs?"

"Scabies . . . Your mamma home?"

Russ pulled back his arm and rubbed it with the palm of his hand. "Naw, she aint."

"It needs attention. Does she know about this?"

"Could be she does." He looked up at Will and then down at his own naked feet. In truth, Russ's mother hadn't been home for days and most likely hadn't looked at her son long enough, in the time that she had been home, to notice anything about him, beyond the fact that he was there, and maybe not even that much.

She made decent money as a dancer and in some ways was very independent, but in other ways (motherhood, for example) she fell short. Every few days she'd come home and buy some groceries and watch some TV with her son and then, in a day or two, she'd be gone again, usually with a man Russ did not know. It was a routine that could not be sustained. Something was bound to happen.

The Department of Children and Families, on two occasions, had taken Russ away from his mother. The second time, the courts almost did not send him back home, and his mother was nearly incarcerated.

Russ picked up a chalky white rock from the edge of the hard dirt road and examined it. "William, can I stay with you tonight? If there's a hurricane coming, I need to stay with you and your dad tonight." He threw the rock into a thicket of sawgrass next to Will's trailer.

"As long as you don't get too close to me," said Will. "Them things is contagious." He mussed Russ's hair a little and then gave him a playful slap on the back of his head.

"I won't give you none," said Russ.

Will took Russ inside and into his dad's bathroom where he found some lotion that his mother had left behind in the medicine cabinet. Will handed Russ the lotion and told him to rub it on his arms. Russ did and he said it made the itching go away some, and it made his arms feel cool.

They went into the living room and turned on the TV. Will wanted to see if the weatherman had anything new to say about the hurricane. His timing was perfect: just as the screen brightened the weatherman pointed at a wall-sized map with a large radar image of a swirling mass of clouds on it. The swirling mass appeared to be headed right towards their part of Florida. Next, on a different map of the same area, there was a computer-generated image of the hurricane, a small iconic symbol, a circle with a hole in the middle of it, like a donut, with two tapered arms stabbing out from it in opposite directions. A widening yellow swath, a path, projected out from the small toy hurricane towards the slightly larger state of Florida. The weather man pointed at this sanitized version of the hurricane and then hovered his hand over the yellow projection, calling it the Cone of Possibility.

Russ scratched his left arm.

"You need to try not to scratch, Russ. Your gonna make it worse."

"You think that storm'll hit us?"

"I don't know. Seems like Sahwoklee County is right in the middle of that cone, and Marshallsville is right in the middle of Sahwoklee. I think we got a pretty good chance. I almost kind of want it to. Don't you, Russ?"

"I hope it does. I hope it comes and blows most of it away."

Will thought that was sad, hearing a little boy say something like that. But he understood, too.

"When's your daddy gitting home? I'm hungry."

"Not for a while, yet."

Russ left-hooked the air and tried to look quarrelsome. "I wish your mom was still around. She'd make us up something hot to eat."

To this, Will said nothing, but his saying nothing sent a message to Russ that he didn't want him bringing up his mother anymore. They both sat silent for a few minutes.

"We can go over to Scotty's," Will finally said, "and see what they got over there in their freezer."

"Yeah! Their mom buys enough food for months." Russ jumped up from the couch.

Will looked at the clock on the wood-paneled wall. "Scotty and Timmy should be home from school by now. Let's go."

Scotty, at sixteen, was short, but wiry and physically strong. He was a running back on the high school football team and was good at it. Despite coming from a poor family and living in an undesirable part of town, and despite being possessed of a somewhat cruel sense of humor, he was popular at school. And even though he was not handsome in the conventional ways, his sturdiness and ebullience deemphasized his less flattering features (a bulbous nose, too big for his face, and thick, tiny ears) and possibly made him appear more handsome than he actually was. In many ways, he was the sort of boy that other boys secretly wanted to be like, a rare figure in the trailer park he and his brother lived in. Will neither liked nor disliked Scotty, though at times he found himself leaning towards the latter.

Timmy, the kinder of the two, was twelve and already taller than his older brother. But he was thin and frail-looking and awkward, and when Will spent too much time around him, he began to feel awkward too.

The brothers' trailer was a short walk up Will's street to the first intersecting road, then a right, and then all the way at the end, a cul-de-sac of some of the nicer yards in the neighborhood. When Will and Russ got to their lot, the brothers were already outside, in the front yard. Scotty was by the front door, pointing an air rifle at Timmy, who had a big red apple on his head. Just as Will and Russ got to the end of the driveway, a big chunk of the left side of the apple exploded and Timmy flinched the other way, and the rest of the apple fell to the ground.

"Sheeee-iiit," said Timmy, with a full-body shiver.

"See, I didn't hitcha." said Scotty. "Did I?" He turned to Will.

"I don't know, but you damn sure blowed the side of it off." Will walked over to the apple and picked it up and examined it.

"You hear about that hurricane?" said Timmy, picking apple debris out of his greasy hair and off his shoulders. "They was talking about it at school. They gave us tomorrow off because it's probably coming this way."

"Russ is gonna stay at our place tonight."

"You aint leaving town?" said Scotty. He was pumping the lever of his air rifle.

"I don't think so," said Will. He looked down at Russ, who was picking at a scab on his arm. "We aint got nowhere to go anyway."

"Our mom said that we was gonna leave if it got to where it looked like it would hit. Our granny lives in South Georgia, in Valdosta, in a real house," said Scotty. He lifted the air rifle up and pointed it at his brother.

"Quit playing," said Timmy.

Scotty pulled the trigger.

There was a low, quick pop and then Timmy hit the ground, holding his face.

They all ran over to Timmy, curled up on the ground, both his hands over his mouth. He was quiet, and his eyes were shut. The rest of the boys, huddled around Timmy, were quiet too. After a short time Timmy got up, and the boys backed away from him.

He stood there in the grassy yard with his right hand over his mouth. He glared at Scotty with the concentration of a wild animal.

Scotty, looking more curious than concerned, moved closer to him. "Take your hand away so I can see."

Timmy took his hand away. The pellet had hit just between his bottom lip and his chin where there was a speck of blood.

They all stood in front of Timmy, in a line, as if he was choosing up sides for kickball.

"Scotty, you shot your brother, man," said Will.

Scotty looked at Will and then back at Timmy. Russ was staring at Timmy, too.

"Shut up, Will," said Scotty.

"You shot him in the face." He pointed at Timmy. He wanted to get angry, but he didn't feel strongly enough about either of the brothers to get worked up. As it was, he only felt shocked. He'd known Scotty was mean, but it hadn't ever occurred to him that he was capable of intentionally shooting his own brother in the face, even if it was only with an air rifle.

"I didn't mean to," said Scotty.

"The hell you didn't," said Will. "You pointed the damn thing right at him and aimed it and all."

"Shut up, Will," said Scotty, again.

"No, you shut up!" said Timmy. He rubbed a finger on the spot where Scotty had shot him. It was red and swollen already, and bled a little. "Oh shit," he said. "It's still in there!"

"No it aint," said Scotty.

"Bullshit it aint!" said Timmy. "Feel it."

Scotty put his hand out and felt the spot with his finger. He felt the perfect little thing under his brother's skin. He smirked and pressed on it.

"Shit, take it easy, asshole. It hurts."

Scotty removed his hand and stepped back. "You can't tell mom about this."

"We got to. She'll be able to get it out."

"Yeah, and she'll beat hell outta both of us, too. She'll beat hell outta me for doing it, but she'll beat hell outta you for letting me do it. Plus, she'll pour alcohol all over ya and take pliers out and dig around in your face until she gets it out—only she'll do it extra long, just to be mean, to teach you a lesson not to ever do it again, and your whole face will turn red from the alcohol and digging around in it with pliers. Naw, we can't tell her."

"Don't you think your mom's gonna wonder what happen to Timmy's face?" said Will.

"We'll have to make something up," said Scotty. He turned to his brother with a mock look of sympathy. "Timmy, think of the pain she'll cause to your face."

"How are we gonna get the pellet out without mom's help?" said Timmy.

"Hell, I can get it out of there," said Scotty.

"Screw that," said Timmy. "I'd rather it stay in there than let you get near it again." He put his finger on the spot.

Just then it started to rain a little and a quick breeze came out of the west and tumbled some of the crisp, brown leaves on the ground. It was late September and some of the trees had already lost all their leaves, despite the heat, or perhaps because of it, like taking off a layer of clothing.

"That's the front of that storm coming," said Russ. "It's coming early."

"Naw," said Will, "It's just a little shower." He looked down at Russ, standing next to him like a little brother. "Scotty, you got any a them frozen dinners in yer freezer?"

Scotty came towards them. "You aint got nothing to eat yourselfs?" He looked down at the rifle on the ground and then over at his wounded brother.

"My dad aint home from work yet and there's no food in the house. I aint hungry, but poor old Russ here aint ate no breakfast or lunch."

Scotty went inside and found some frozen burritos in the freezer and grabbed a couple and gave them to Will and Russ.

The two boys started back towards Will's trailer. The wind was picking up, sweet and cool. Wind from someplace else, thought Will. A nicer place. Any place is a nicer place. He felt like dreaming up visions of places he could go to; he wanted to conjure up images of towns and scenarios of himself interacting with strange, new people, in new ways, but he couldn't. He only thought about the hurricane and poor old Timmy, having to live with such a shitty brother, and poor old Russ, with such a shitty mom. Plus, he didn't really know any other places. He only knew this place, these people. Sure, he knew the names of places and he'd been to a few other towns in Central Florida, but they were all more or less just like Marshallsville: trailer parks, truck stops, orange groves, packing houses…. Anything he might have imagined would have only looked like Marshallsville and would have only included these people, the people in his life, and, of course, his mother, who was no longer physically in his life, but who was there, in his mind, and would have surely been in these longed for images and scenarios had he the ability to imagine them. She'd have been there, walking down a street, or sitting at a table in the window of a diner, folding clothes in a Laundromat, somewhere. Only he couldn't quite picture any of it, so she just floated there in his mind, like she was nowhere.

He unlocked the front door, opened it, and hurried Russ in, and then locked the door behind them. Inside, he put the frozen burritos in the microwave and got out plates and forks and a bottle of hot sauce from the fridge. Once the burritos were ready they ate them quickly, and were done in just a few minutes.

"I'm still hungry. That burrito just angered my belly."

"I know. Me, too. My dad will be home soon though. He'll take us somewhere to get something."

Will got up and looked out the kitchen window. It was raining steadily now. Occasionally there was a flash of lightning followed by a low rumble. The thunder was soothing to Will. It made him feel good. It even comforted him a little, like reassuring words. From the window, he watched Scotty and Timmy's mom's blue LTD turn onto their street. She took the turn quickly, making the tires screech. He knew his dad would be pulling in soon, too.

He turned from the window and his disappointing thoughts to see what Russ was doing. He'd heard him in the background, clanking around the kitchen.

Russ was back at the small dinner table with a cereal bowl in front of him. He was slurping liquid from a spoon. Will walked over to Russ, who was now grinning and holding the spoon above the bowl with his left hand.

"There aint nothing in that bowl but ice and water."

Russ slurped a spoonful. "It's delicious."

"Have you lost your mind?"

"It's something I made. It's a special meal." He slurped again and closed his eyes and moaned. "It's so good."

"I guess you're a big fan of ice water."

"This aint ice water."

"Well, what is it then?"

"This here's arctic soup."

"Arctic soup?"

"Yes. An Eskimo showed it to me."

He's lost it, thought Will. "Well, then. Can you make me up some too?" He figured that playing along would help pass the time.

"No. But you can make your own self up some. It's easy. It's basically just ice water in a bowl."

Will heard a vehicle pull into the carport.

"Boys," said Sam, Will's dad, as he climbed through the front door of the trailer. Will's dad was a fuller version of Will, an older model. They looked just alike in most ways. They were the same height and had the same build, tall and thin. Their faces were even almost the same, except Will's was smother and thinner and younger. Also there was something in Will's face that was absent from his father's: a wildness that seemed to be located in his eyes, or thereabouts—one of his mother's few contributions to his physical appearance. He sat down next to Russ and looked into his bowl. "Whatcha eating there, Russ?"

"Arctic soup, or iceberg stew, whichever. A Eskimo told it to me."

"Oh, looks good." He glanced at Will. Will grinned.

Sam noticed Russ's arms and scooted his chair a couple of inches away from him. He looked at Will. Will nodded.

"Why didn't you go to work today, son?" He stood up and started unbuttoning his shirt. It had a patch on the right breast that read Sam.

"I wasn't feeling good."

"That's twiced in two weeks. They're gonna fire you if you keep it up." He threw his shirt on the back of the chair he'd been sitting in. He kept on his white undershirt.

"I know. I been thinking of leaving, though."

"Yeah, where you going?"

"I don't know." He paused and locked eyes with his dad. "Maybe wherever mom went."

"Where's that?" He grabbed the back of the chair, resting the weight of the top of his body on it.

"I bet it's better than here, wherever it is." He looked at Russ who seemed to be listening to every word.

"I guess that wouldn't be too hard to manage," said Sam. He put his head down for a few seconds and then pushed himself away from the chair he'd been holding onto.

"What you say we go get something to eat and discuss this here storm?" He looked at Russ. "That is unless you're filled up on that Es-kee-mo soup."

"No," said Russ, "I'm hungry for some real food. Eskimos don't eat real filling foods."

They piled into Sam's pickup truck and drove through the rain to Dan's Drive-in and got burgers and sat in the truck and ate and talked about what to do about the hurricane. They decided that they'd all three stay in the trailer and ride it out. "It's a category 3," said Will's dad, "but we won't get a direct hit. I'm pretty sure of that. If we stay out of the bedrooms and the kitchen, unless we really need to, and stay in the living room, in the middle of the trailer, we'll be okay. I've been through this kind of thing before. It's no big deal. Besides, it'll be like camping." He looked over at Russ and smiled. "We can even set up a tent in the living room."

Russ jumped in the small back seat of the extended cab and said, "Yes! Let's set up a tent."

"Scotty and Timmy said that they'd be going to their granny's up in Georgia," said Will. "Nan and Pa, live over in the panhandle. We could drive over and stay with them for the night. We'd be a lot safer there."

"I'm glad them boys got somewhere to go, but we won't need to go nowhere. We'll be fine."

Will didn't want to argue. Ultimately, he trusted his father's assessment of the storm. Really, he'd just been interested in gauging his dad's reaction to the suggestion of staying at his mom's parent's house. Ever since his mother's disappearance, Nan and Pa had been antagonistic towards Will's dad. Naturally, they were worried about their only daughter, and didn't quite believe that Sam didn't know where she was. The first few months, they'd called regularly, and Sam always, out of respect, told them everything he knew, which was nothing, and each time they had not been satisfied. These calls had upset Will in a complicated way. He didn't like the way his grandparents treated his father, but he also shared their frustration. He wanted to know where his mother was, too—just as badly as his grandparents, he wanted to know, and it was all too easy for him—like his grandparents—to heap all the blame for his not knowing on his father. It hadn't occurred to any of them, it seemed, that Sam wanted to know where she was too.

They finished their food and then Will's dad drove them to the hardware store and bought a few things, a couple flashlights, batteries, and some candles and five jugs of water. They were lucky that there were any emergency supplies left at the store. They were lucky, in fact, said the cashier, that they'd made it before the store closed.

"You aint leaving town?" said the cashier, a boy, about sixteen, with braces on his teeth and thick red hair. He was wearing a red vest, with a name tag that read Jeffrey.

"Nope," said Will. "You leaving?"

"Naw, we don't live near no water. Plus, my dad says it aint gonna be a direct hit. Just get some rain and wind from some of the bands. He said it'll be like getting a tropical storm is all."

Will looked at his dad and they smiled at each other.

By the time they got back to their trailer it was raining hard. They pulled into the carport and found Scotty, Timmy, and their mom, standing next to the front door, wet and mopey looking.

"What you doing in the carport, Lydia?" said Will's dad.

The boys' mother explained in her South Georgia drawl: "Sam, that storm's coming and seems like we aint gonna be able ta get to my mom's in Valdosta and… shoot, I barely made it home, because my car was overheating and I couldn't stop….I was running red lights and stop signs….And I got home and them boys was up ta something." She took a moment to look at both of them. "I aint sure exactly what they's up ta, but Timmy has that Band Aid on his face." She pointed over to Timmy, black hair dangling down over his face, standing next to his shorter, sturdier brother. His bottom lip was swollen and there was a tiny Band Aid just under it, making it look like a patched tire. "They aint said what caused it, but it can't be good. So, anyways, Sam, I was hoping maybe we could come stay with y'all ta ride this thing out, just over night, till it's gone."

Sam smiled and laughed a little at the sight of the boys and their exasperated mother. "Yeah, that's fine, Lydia. We got the room. We'll just spread everbody out."

They all went inside and, while everyone stood in the kitchen, Will and Sam started setting things up. Will went through all the closets getting blankets and sheets and pillows, and towels for Lydia and her boys, and Sam set up the new candles in different areas of the trailer, and then put batteries into all the flashlights, and retrieved the candles left over from last hurricane season.

Tired of watching while Sam and Will worked, Lydia volunteered to go fill the bathtub with water. "You gotta have a tub a water, just in case. You never know how bad these things is gonna get."

"Yep," said Sam. "That's good thinking. I forgot about that." He was now busy putting up the small tent in the middle if the living room. Russ helped.

Sam noticed that Russ was still scratching. Damn, he thought. We should have stopped and got Russ some medicine. "Russ," he said, "You feeling all right?"

"Itches." He stopped and itched to prove his point.

"What's wrong with him?" said Lydia, who was back in the living room, after scrubbing the tub clean for the water they'd soon fill it with.

"He's got scabies," said Sam.

"Scabies?" She got down on her knees and pulled Russ toward her and looked at his arms. "Your mamma know about this?"

He started to cry.

"I reckon not," said Lydia. She pulled Russ close to her and hugged him. "I got some cream to the house that'll help some. It won't make them go away but it'll cut down on the itching until you can get some proper medicine."

"I'll go get it," said Will.

"The hell you will," said Lydia. "Scotty, get your ass up and go get that cream. It's in my medicine cabinet. It's the only thing in there in a tube, other than the toothpaste."

"Why I gotta go? What's scabies?"

"Because I said so, and because you done something to your little brother. I don't know what, but—"

"He shot him with a pellet gun," said Russ, still crying, still huddled close to Lydia.

Will sputtered with laughter.

"You what?" She stood and turned toward Scotty, keeping one hand on Russ's shoulder.

"No, I aint done it." He looked at Russ, astounded.

"Yes he did," said Timmy, crying now, too. "He shot me just for the curiousness of it."

Lydia let go of Russ and walked toward Scotty, who was sitting at one of the dinner table chairs, slumped over just enough to properly pout. There was a hint of shame in his look. Despite being a total jerk, he knew he'd done something cruel, and he could see a large measure of his cruelty in the faces of everyone in the trailer. His mother stood over him.

"You get your ass up and go get that medicine, boy." Her hands were fists.

"Yessum." Scotty got up and walked out the door into the rain.

She shook her head and turned around.

Will looked out the window. "You want me to run and catch up with him, make sure he makes it all right?"

Sam started to say, yes, but Lydia said, "No, he'll be fine. A little rain never hurt nobody." Then she went over to Timmy. "Come here, son. Let me see your lip."

Timmy started crying again, thinking of pliers and having his face doused with alcohol. But there were no pliers, and the boy's mother, using eyelash tweezers, gently and with extreme care removed the pellet from her sons face before her other son had the chance to return with the cream for Russ's arms. And there was no alcohol either. But there was hydrogen peroxide, instead, which, to Timmy's delight, didn't burn nearly as much.

After things were settled and Lydia was through talking to her sons about how things were hard enough without them "behaving like little heathen bastards half the time," they all gathered in the living room to watch the TV, to see where the storm was, to see how close it had come during the last couple hours.

The storm had spun its way a few hundred miles closer, and the predicted path had been shifted a little north, so that the worst-case scenario, to the extreme left of the cone, put the storm's eye right on Marshallsville. "Most likely," said Sam, "it'll pass a little north of us and we'll get some weather—some wind—It's a Cat 3 so we can expect for things to get beat up a bit and blown around. Rain, too. We'll get a few inches—but I don't think we're gonna see a lot of serious flooding, maybe just in some of the low lying areas."

Will, sitting on the couch, next to Russ, let his thoughts rest again on his own mother. He thought about the Cone of Possibility, applying it to his mother: the longer she was gone, the farther from home she got, the less likely she'd return. In his mind he created a scene like that of a TV news room, a huge map of the southeastern states, longitude and latitude lines going through it. He pictured, instead of a little hurricane symbol, an icon of a woman (like the ones on restroom doors), facing north, positioned to stroll right out of Florida. In front of her, signifying her possible paths, was the Cone of Possibility. The further out it spread, the wider it got, until it became a wide yellow circle going completely around the little woman, until, finally, the circle got so wide it covered everything, every part of the map.

A bright flash of light brought him out of his daydreaming, then darkness, then a thunder clap so loud he couldn't hear for a few seconds after.

"There goes the power," said Sam. "Will, help me light all the candles."

Will and his dad went around the trailer lighting candles and moving them around. They put two in the kitchen, one in the hall bathroom, and three in the living room—one on the coffee table in front of the couch, one across the room, on top of the TV, and one by the window, on a small table. As Will put the one by the window he saw how bad it had got outside.

"It sure is raining out there. Windy too."

The rest of the boys crowded around the window and looked out.

"Dang," said Russ. "The top of that scrubby pine in the back is just about touching the ground." He scratched his right arm for emphasis.

"Look at your trailer!" said Scotty. He elbowed Russ.

The aluminum siding on Russ's trailer had peeled halfway off on the right side and was lashing in the wind. As they watched, it peeled more and eventually came completely off and flew away, almost hitting Will's trailer.

"Damn," said Scotty. His mom slapped him on the back of his head.

"At least no one's in there," said Lydia.

"Yeah." Sam looked at Russ. "You okay, boy?"

"I'm itching," he said.

Russ looked tired. It had been a long day. "Let Ms. Lydia put some more cream on ya and then try going to bed. Okay?"

Russ looked up at Sam with something like a look of gratitude.

"Yessir," he said and left the room with Lydia.

In an hour everyone was asleep but Will and Sam. Will sat watching the candle on the TV, and listening to the rain, that had by now become nothing more than an awkward drizzle.

"It's about passed," said Sam. "We've seen the worst of it." He smoothed his hand over the velvety couch cushion next to him.

Will got up and walked over to the window. It was just a matter of time until it was quiet and still again, back to normal. But he wasn't sure he wanted that. In fact, the more he thought about it, the less he wanted it. But what else was there? He looked at Russ's trailer, battered but still there. He turned from the window and looked at his dad, sitting on the couch, with his head down now, asleep. He walked over and sat next to him. He grabbed a blanket from the arm of the couch, unfolded it and covered up with it. Within a few minutes he was asleep.

Jimmie & Lester

Jimmie sitting on an overturned bucket with her knees apart and I can see up her shorts. It's been a good long while. But I know what the answer is. No need to ask. Been in the high nineties for a week straight. We ain't bathed for days. I decide to take a quick dip in the retention pond next to the strip mall on the other side of the woods we sitting in, and we strip and run in, rub down and scratch the filth loose, run back into the woods. Jimmie giggles the whole time. She's got lots of laughter in her. I keep looking. I get the feeling somebody seen us. We dry off and get dressed. After setting quiet for a while we gather up our shit and walk to a deeper clearing in the woods to be safe. We put our blankets down on the ground and sit. I been doing this almost all my life. Not Jimmie though.

I'm almost all the way dry, except for my hair. Jimmie sleeping on her blanket, her damp hair up in a towel like a mom or a wife. It starts to sprinkle. Your usual Florida summer afternoon shower. But I don't feel any of the raindrops. It gets to where it's raining hard, and I can hear it hissing and thumping onto the tops of the trees, but I don't feel a single drop, and the sound of it overhead makes the woods feel busy and alive. It calms me. I lie down and close my eyes and listen. I could be lulled to sleep this way. But I don't really sleep. I haven't had a good hard sleep in years. Finally I open my eyes and sit up.

"Jim," I say. I walk over to her and look at her face. She looks peaceful. But she's hanging out of her top. I wonder how she can sleep like that. It's strange how a person can get used to things being wrong or a little off. I want to touch it. I think about putting my mouth on it. I bend down and reach my hand out.

"What are you doing?" she says. She don't move. Her light blue eyes is on me.

"Trying to wake you up. It's raining."

She cups her breast back into her shirt. She pulls back her scraggily brown hair and makes a harsh sound in her throat and spits something compact and heavy off into the woods.

I walk back to the bucket I been sitting on.

"I don't know how many times we've been over this." She stands up and stretches.

I shift my weight on the bucket, rock it back and forth.

"We're too close." She rifles through her army bag, looking for something. Homeless folks is always looking for shit that's long gone. "We're best friends. I care about you too much." She pauses, looks up from the bag.

"I care about you too. That's all the more reason. It's like you teasing me, lying around half-exposed."

"How about Anita? She'll do it for free. She likes you." She pulls a tiny empty bottle from her bag.

"Anita?"

"What's wrong with Anita?"

"Well, she could use a trip to the dentist, for starters. Plus she's always scratching at herself."

"Anita doesn't have anything—communicable." She pulls another small bottle from her bag and drinks what little bit is inside of it, throws it into some nearby underbrush.

"I know she don't. I just ain't interested in Anita."

"Quiet," says Jimmie. "Hear that?"

I hear voices coming from the woods next to the retention pond. We gather up our things and run off in the opposite direction. Once we figure we're at a safe distance we stop and sit down in a hollow and stay quiet for a while.

I don't know exactly how Jimmie ended up like this, but I've pieced some things together over the years. No one out here knows her better than me. She used to teach—at a high school, I believe. She was married. Sometimes she says, "He was a very decent man," or "He was a devoted husband and a good father." She never says nothing about love or that he was handsome or nothing like that, and she never uses his name around me. And I know she has growed-up kids. She sends postcards and letters to "Dearest Christina" and "Dearest Richard." That's all I know for sure. But something went real wrong to put her out here with me. Where are Dearest Christina and Dearest Richard? Wouldn't they come help their mother if they knowed she was out here? Do they know she is out here? Something bad musta happened. The way she talks about them, the tone in her voice. She feels guilt. Maybe she cheated. Maybe he cheated, and she responded violently. But that can't be it. That can't be the only thing. That's not enough to make a woman homeless.

I wake up and Jimmie gone, and her blanket and bag gone too. I figure she off going. "I'm going to potty," she'll say. Nobody says "potty" unless they raised children. I stand up and stretch and smell myself under the arms. Then I hear something. I think it's probably Jimmie coming back from going, but it ain't.

I say, "Jimmie," just louder than a whisper. I hear some laughter a ways off and walk in that direction. I hear underbrush being disturbed and some more laughing, and I start to see something other than the greens and browns of the woods. I see reds and blues and flesh. I move behind a tree.

I see some boys, four boys. They on their knees, huddled up around something like around a campfire, but the one in front of me has his pants down around his knees, and he is leaned over, holding up the top of his body with his bare arms, and I see two long skinny legs sticking out to the sides of the boy's body, coming out from under him, and I can tell they Jimmie's legs.

I don't know what to do, but when I watch the boy in front of me get up and pull his pants back on, and the boy to his left get up and take down his pants and get down on his knees, where the first boy was, I know I need to do something.

But I don't. I can't move. I ain't scared, and I ain't interested in watching. I'm just stuck somehow. My body won't move.

The second boy slaps hands with the boy to his right and he howls. I look around and see a club-sized stick on the ground about six feet from me. I could pick it up and run over there and clobber the shit out of one of them and the rest of them would probably scatter. Hell, the sight of me alone would probably be enough to make them run. Still, I don't move.

"Turn over, turn over!" says the one in front of me, and I can't believe it, because she does. She turns right goddamn over. For a second, I almost get mad at Jimmie, then I shake that thought off.

I crawl over and grab the stick. One of the boys say he hears something and they all stop and glance around for a moment, but I don't move. The third one gets up and starts undoing his pants, and I get up too, and once he has his pants down, I come at them, yelling.

He turns around and looks at me and I can see his eyes, and they're frightened and maybe humiliated. The other boys run off into the woods, and I bring that stick down on his head, straight down, and he falls, stays there for a few seconds and then gets up, tugging at his pants and trying to run and crying all at once. Jimmie lay there void of emotion, drained of it, or in a place beyond it.

"Jimmie," I say. She don't answer, but her eyes is wide open, and I watch her blink a couple times. And her eyes look like they staring at something inward. I sit down next to her head. I do not dare touch her. I pick up a twig and twirl it with my finger and thumb.

After a moment, she curls up like a little girl and I get up and get her ratty pink blanket and put it over her.

I think about asking her if she all right or if I can get her something, but I don't, because she ain't all right and there ain't nothing I can get her. I figure the best thing I can do is just sit here and keep an eye on her, try to make her feel safe. After a while she closes her eyes and goes to sleep.

I think about them boys. They got mamas and daddies and maybe even sisters. It's not hard to imagine. They might sit at a dinner table tonight and eat tuna casserole and drink a glass of milk. One might watch a baseball game with his dad. One might say good night to his mama and kiss his little sister on the head. And what will they think of this monstrous thing they did? What will they think of Jimmie? They will carry this with them for the rest of their lives. If there is any decency in them, they could be ruined by this. A part of me—most of me— hopes they will be.

I don't know what Jimmie did to end up out here. She might tell me someday, but whatever she did, she don't deserve this.

I walk back to where our things is and gather it all up and bring it over to where Jimmie is. I lay out my blanket next to her and sit down on it. I get the beef jerky out of my bag and sit there chewing, watching Jimmie sleep, and soon it starts to rain again. I can hear the rain drops hitting the roof of the wood, that nice hissing sound. But, again, I don't feel a single drop. Not one drop hits me the whole time I sit there with Jimmie. Except for that hissing sound on top of the trees, it's like it ain't even happening.

The Tattler

A massive live oak stood on either side of the entrance to Hatfield Estates Retirement Village. Their highest branches reached across the boulevard, into each other, creating a canopy under which Delmer Blevins now stood in the mottled shade waiting for his little sister's school bus to peek over Grab-All Hill to the north on County Road 304. His little sister, Lila, called the two old trees Buford and Brutus, and they were as distinct as people to her. She'd climb them and talk to them, and once she was well into the dense top of one it was nearly impossible to get her down. She'd sit with her assortment of naked and half-clothed Barbie dolls and spend hours laying out static little scenarios with them. She didn't give them the most eventful lives, but they were always a family—mom, dad, sister and big brother—and they'd have dinner and play games and watch TV, always together, always doing things that Lila could still barely remember her own family doing. Other times she'd just sit as high as she could climb, her skinny body sprawled across a thick limb, and stare out over the tops of the cars flying by and think about the state of things in her own static life.

Lila hopped off the bus heavy with the day's entanglements—pink backpack, orange safety patrol belt, a gray sweat shirt rolled up and tied around her waist, and a bright green science-project poster board under her arm. She walked over to Delmer and he unburdened her of the poster board.

"Well," she began, "I don't advance to the finals."

Delmer unfolded the poster board and took a look at his sister's work. He'd helped some, mostly with the gluing and cutting and the layout, but she'd done all the research herself. He was proud of her for that. She was not a lazy child. On the back of the poster board, in the bottom-left corner, in red ink, was printed *A- Great Job, Lila!!!*

"I think you done a real nice job of it."

"Not finals nice."

"Don't matter," said Delmer, hung-over and not in the mood for elaboration of any kind. The night before he and his good friend Lucien Nix had each made empty four quarts of King Cobra malt liquor while shooting at stop signs and billboards with Lucien's two new handguns. As they rounded the left turn onto their street he glanced back toward the entry where a Sahwoklee Regional Utilities truck was backing in. There'd been a thunderstorm two nights before and the electricity had gone out in the whole park. Lila had gotten scared and Delmer ended up reading to her by candlelight from her favorite book, *Peter Pan,* until the electricity came back on.

Lila talked the entire way home. "Well," she began, as if in response to something Delmer had already said, "this black boy, Lionel Young, was running down the main hall by the resources wing and I told him to stop running and he stuck out his middle finger at me." She paused. "So I reported him."

"Tattler," said Delmer.

Lila stuck her tongue out at him. "I'm a patrol. I'm supposed to tattle." She put her hand on her orange safety patrol belt.

"Keep going," said Delmer.

"Well, he got a detention, and as we were leaving principal McGregor's office, he called me a name I'd never heard before, but it sounded really bad."

Delmer didn't bother asking Lila what the boy had called her. He didn't really care, and he didn't feel like struggling to explain God only knew what.

"Well, he probably likes you. That's what boys his age do when they like you."

Lila tilted her head, considering the suggestion, then shook it off. "I can't imagine ever liking anybody new anymore—not for a good long while."

Besides their grandmother, Lucy Nugent, Delmer and Lila had one other living relative, an uncle, whose name was Goad Blevins, who lived in Cortez, the next town over. After the accident, he had not been deemed a fit guardian, which was why they lived with their grandmother. Goad owned a bar and was not married, had had polio as a child and walked with a pronounced limp. Though the limp was noticeable it did not seem to slow him down much. He was, in fact, able to achieve a quick—albeit hard to watch—sprint, and was more agile than most when doing certain things, like tending bar. In the end, the judge had thought the grandmother a better fit for them. But because Hatfield Estates was a retirement community, the judge had had to issue a court order to allow the children to live there temporarily until something better could be arranged. It was a nice place, but neither Delmer nor Lila particularly liked it there. No one talked to them except their grandmother and a smiley old widower named Buddy who lived next door. Everyone else either ignored them all together or sneered at them and made faces. Sometimes they'd even say things around them, like, "Children aren't even supposed to be living here," as if Delmer and Lila didn't already know it.

Delmer made Lila a snack of buttered toast, her favorite, and one of the only non-sweet things she'd eat without a fuss. Their grandma was away for the afternoon, and it was just them.

"Uncle Goad said he'd pick me up a little early so we can go to Dino's before the movie."

Delmer walked to the kitchen window and pushed aside the little lacey curtain. If he strained, he could just hear the utility truck's diesel engine idling. He was pretty sure he knew what they were going to do.

"I can taste it now," said Lila. She examined her plate, littered with dark brown bread crusts and black crumbs. "He always lets me order the banana split. No one else ever does. He's the only one. Mom and dad never even did."

Delmer heard a high-pitched whine rip through the air and then die down to a stuttering rumble just above the sound of the truck's engine.

"You still got about an hour yet before he gets here. You got any homework to knock out before he does?"

"No homework on Fridays, dummy. Last time I got nuts, but this time I think I'll say no nuts because it kind of drowns out the flavors of the other stuff."

Lila got up and put her plate of bread husks on the kitchen counter. Delmer heard the high-pitched whine again, but this time it lasted longer and was more violent sounding: a saw ripping into a tree branch. Lila squinted and angled her head towards the window.

"What's that?"

"Just someone doing yard work." He didn't want to lie to her, but he didn't want her freaking out either. She could really lose it when she wanted to. She'd scream and thrash and cuss. On more than a few occasions Delmer had heard Lila use cuss words he didn't even use. He figured once Goad arrived, he could pull him aside for a moment, before they left for the movies, and tell him to take the construction access road in the back of the park and she'd never know the difference.

Lila shrugged and walked toward her room. Delmer told her to get cleaned up and to change out of her school clothes.

When Goad finally arrived Delmer had Lila go get her science project to show her uncle. She rolled her eyes, moaned, and walked like a zombie into her room to get it.

"Don't know if you noticed there," Delmer said, once she was out of earshot, "but utility company come out to trim up those big oaks out front. Other night the electricity went out when a limb broke loose of one and knocked out a power line."

Goad said that he had noticed the utility vehicle.

"If Lila sees that, she'll go ape shit crazy on you. You ought to take the back way out of the neighborhood."

"What does she care?"

"She loves them trees, man. She got names for them and everything. I'll tell her tomorrow, but there's no reason for her night to be ruined."

Goad agreed, and when Lila returned with her science project he made a big deal out of looking at it, taking his reading glasses out of his breast pocket and examining it for a good long time. "Oo-wee," he said. "Would you look at this here?" He told her how crazy the judges had been not to select it for the finals.

"I don't even understand half of what you got wrote down on this thing." He winked at Delmer and slapped his back. "Welp, we got banana splits calling our names."

Once they were gone, Delmer walked back to the entrance to assess the damage. It was quiet out now. All the old fogies were either asleep or fixing to be. They'd done a superb hack job on the trees. The canopy, the whole leafy embrace of it, was completely gone. All the limbs that had reached over and into each other had been amputated nearly to the trunk. They'd pruned the very top limbs into an uneven v-shape around the power lines, and all the lower limbs were cut back so excessively that there weren't really any climbing limbs left. The combined effect of it all was such that the once magnificent twins now looked solitary and abused and withdrawn. It was disrespectful, he thought. A violence had been done to the trees. They'd taken no care at all. It made him mad. Lila's gonna flip, he thought. People just do things, he said to himself as he walked back to his granny's trailer.

The next morning Delmer lay in bed listening to his grandmother in the kitchen. She was watching TV and doing dishes. He heard her say, "Suits me. I never liked her character anyway." After a few minutes she said, "Well, good morning, Ms. Lila," in a high, excited voice.

This is not so bad, he thought. Things could be much worse. Delmer enjoyed lying there in bed eavesdropping on the tiny world around him, letting the day slowly brighten. The night before, once Lucy had made it home, Delmer had walked the three miles to Lucien's and they'd messed around some more with the handguns. Lucien lived on thirty acres of nicely wooded land and they'd set up some beer bottles and cans as targets and shot and drank beer for a good while. Lucien sneaked his dad's truck keys and gave Delmer a ride home at around two-thirty in the morning.

He listened to bits of talk: Lila telling Lucy about her night with Goad, about the movie they'd seen, and about banana splits, hers with no nuts, and about how she'd probably go back to nuts, because it'd seemed like something was missing. She told her grandmother about her science project and Lionel, the bad boy at school who'd called her a bad name. On and on she went, as she was prone to do. Eventually Delmer quit listening and got out of bed and began thinking about how he was going to break it to Lila about the trees.

Lucy had made biscuits and scrambled eggs and bacon, the remains of which were laid out on the stove top. Delmer made a plate and sat down at the table in the kitchen, next to Lila, who was pushing a last lump of scrambled egg onto a fork with her finger.

Delmer asked her if she'd liked the movie. She said she had. "Uncle Goad fell asleep about twenty minutes into it, though, like he always does."

"Always?" said Lucy as she put her plate into the sink.

"Mostways," said Lila.

Delmer told Lila that after she'd finished eating and brushed her teeth and gotten dressed he wanted to show her something, which was probably a mistake, because it made her so curious that she bugged him with questions the whole time he was eating.

He was done getting ready first and he waited in the kitchen for Lila.

"What're we doing?" she said as she walked into the kitchen.

"There's something you need to see."

"What?" she said.

"Just come on." He took up her hand and they walked out of the trailer and down the road toward the park entrance. It was already hot out. Buddy, their friendly neighbor was out in his yard, pruning his hedges. He stopped and waved at the two as they passed. They both waved back and kept going. Buddy stood and watched them, smiling, until they rounded the bend and he could no longer see them.

Once they were close enough to the entrance that you could just see the trees, Delmer stopped, whirled Lila around, and grabbed her by the shoulders.

"There's something you need to see and you ain't gonna like it," he said.

She just stared up at Delmer. He turned her around and pointed towards the two mangled trees. She walked forward, looking.

"What happened?" She held one hand up over her eyes.

"The utility workers came and pruned em up."

"Why?"

"Remember when the electricity went out two nights ago?"

"Yes."

"It was the trees that caused it, so they had to cut them back. They had to do it. They'd got too big."

She pointed up at the power line. "They cut them back too far."

"Well, they had to do it that way so they wouldn't have to come back for a while."

"It looks like they didn't take their time with it. They could have done it so they'd look nice."

"I guess they had other things they needed to get to."

Lila slapped her hands against her thighs, and then, as casual as anything, said what might be described as a very obscure cuss word. It took Delmer by surprise and he tried not to laugh. The word was familiar to him, but he could not remember the last time he'd heard someone use it. Maybe he'd never actually heard a person use it. Maybe he'd read it somewhere. Anyway, it seemed to him like a very adult cuss word, one that required a certain degree of verbal acuity to use, unlike most of the ones kids usually tried out on each other. He had no idea where she might have heard it.

"You shouldn't use words like that, Lila." He didn't want to make too big a fuss of it.

"That's what that boy Lionel called me. What's it mean, anyway?"

Delmer could tell she was gearing up for one of her meltdowns: her narrow body was tensed up and she had made tight fists with her delicate fingers. Her hands were their mother's hands. She used to put Lila's hand on hers and say, "It's miraculous, ain't it, Lila? We've got the very same hands!"

"Never mind what it means," said Delmer. "All you need to know is it's an ugly thing to say and I don't ever want to hear you say it again."

"Seems like I don't like what nobody ever does no more," she said.

Hearing his little sister say such a negative thing made Delmer feel depressed.

She let out a long, slow groan. She said the word again, but this time she growled it. The small, dense word tore off her lips with proficiency, as if she'd been using the word all her life. Delmer moved closer to her and put his hand on her shoulder and gently rubbed it. He felt her body shiver, as if she were freezing. He put his arm around her, half embrace and half restraint, and she let out a throaty scream. Delmer picked her up and held onto her tightly. She tried thrashing her body, but Delmer was too strong. In fits she tried to wiggle loose of his grip until finally her small, sweaty body went limp, and she got quiet, her chest heaving with deep, stammering breaths.

Lila and Delmer watched an old man, driving a golf cart, pass by. Lila stuck her tongue out, once he'd passed. "I'm old enough to know what things mean," she said to her brother.

"I know it," said Delmer.

They were sitting almost in the street. Delmer sat cross-legged, holding her the way you hold a baby. He put his hand on her sweaty forehead. It was good to face a thing head on, he thought, so that you could move on with your life. Just bam, then go. She knew how to do that. He'd seen her do it with a thing far more traumatic. "We better head on back now," he said to Lila. He took her under the arms and lifted her off his lap and held her in place like a plank of wood with one hand while he got to his feet. He took her hand, and she did not pull it away, and they turned and quietly walked back toward the trailer. It was morning still, and he was glad for that.

Deek's Philosophies

It got to where I hated him so much that I could hardly stand it. I thought about *losing* him. I thought about dropping him off somewhere, out in the middle of nowhere, where things get lost. I thought about *accidents*. He could get hit by a car. He could get into something, poison. He could *run away* and never come back. I let him out three mornings ago, for some fresh air, I'd say, and he never came back. Something could happen. Things happened all the time.

Three months ago I saw this documentary about this Midwestern town where they have so many stray and feral cats that they pay people to kill them. It's not like they have city employees, on the payroll, that go around killing baby kittens. It's not like that. But there are these people who go around, sort of like the people you see who collect cans on the sides of roads, and look for areas where there are high concentrations of stray and feral cats and they do different things, like lay out poisons and traps. They go back later and see if they have killed or trapped any, and if they have, they bag them up, and take them to a certain location, just like with aluminum cans, and they give them to the attendants and they get paid in cash, per cat. I forget how much. They never said what they do with the cats after they get them. I assume they just throw them away, or incinerate them.

That documentary made me feel a little sick, but I couldn't stop watching it. I didn't like those cat hunters. They were sketchy guys. Of course they were all guys. You didn't see any women doing this. But they did interview the girlfriend of one of them. I guess you'd call this guy the leader. He was tall, and handsome in an I-kill-cats kind of way. Only about twenty-one. Stringy shoulder-length black hair, always wearing the same thing: white sleeveless t-shirt and black denim pants.

They interviewed his girlfriend who was always chewing gum. She was pretty in a my-boyfriend-kills-cats kind of way. She was only sixteen and she said her daddy had moved them up from Georgia for work. She said her father had been transferred from a plastics plant in Georgia to one in the town (I forgot the name) they were in, in Ohio. He was an extrusion welder, she said, whatever that means.

She said that she didn't care what Deek (the name of her cat-killing boyfriend) did as long as he bought her "purdy things". She held up a ring with a *tiny* sparkle in it, and then she kissed it and smiled. She had bad teeth.

The other two cat recyclers were only about eighteen or nineteen and they looked a lot like Deek, except smaller. They all dressed about the same and they shared the same kind of philosophies, Deek's philosophies, about what they did for a living. Stuff like: *These cats are suffering out here on the streets. We're just puttin' 'em out of their misery. And the people of this town. We're helpin' 'em. If it weren't for us these streets would be overrun with cats. And these cats are sick and dangerous. Some of 'em have rabies and other things. Would you want a little kid to get hurt because of one of these things? I wouldn't. They're like rats. Out here, in our town, these things are like rats, or roaches. They're everywhere. We're just doin' the right thing.*

The right thing. It made me think. Was it the right thing? It didn't seem right. It didn't feel right. But maybe the right thing doesn't always feel right. Like when you're a kid, and you know you should tell the truth about something, you know it's the right thing to do, but you just can't bring yourself to do it, so you go ahead with the lie, and it feels good. It feels right. It feels right to do the wrong thing.

Before I was basically forced to take him, I had loved thunderstorms. Now, because of the trauma of that time, I can't stand them. From the first almost inaudible growl of thunder to the last, he howled. If the storm lasted fifteen minutes, he howled for fifteen minutes. If the storm lasted two hours, he howled for two hours. Before him, during thunderstorms, I would drink coffee and read, or just lie on the couch and listen—relax and enjoy the storm. After he arrived, I spent the whole time during a thunderstorm, throwing things at him. I would open the door to the screened-in porch and stand there and throw things at him as he howled at the weather. Empty two-liter bottles, pens, forks, spoons—a meat tenderizer once—a dustpan, old remote controls, books, anything I could think of that wouldn't *really* hurt him. It had become a game, a sick game, and honestly, I was above it.

The problem, essentially, was this: I couldn't get rid of him, and I couldn't keep him. Yes, I hated him, but my girlfriend, my lovely girlfriend, loved him. She loved *Rex*. That's what she called him. Rex. I never named him. I refused to. I just called him, Him. To get rid of him would have meant serious trouble. My girlfriend would have, well, I didn't want to find out what she'd do, but I knew it would have been something tragic, something resulting in me not being with her. And, you see, she *was* truly lovely to me. I felt lucky to have her, because, well, because I'm not what you'd call handsome, and not what you'd call thin or physically fit, and fairly boring (I love board games. She called them "bored" games), so I needed to hold on to her. I needed to keep Rachel. I needed to not piss her off too much. There would be no more Rachels for me. No Sarahs, Julies, Marthas, Belindas, Mollies, Sallies, Keris….This was it. My last chance at snagging a woman.

After the first week I suggested to her that she take him. "Why don't you take him home with you, since you love him so much?" She flipped out. She reminded me about her roommate's allergies and asthma, and she reminded me about their brand new carpet, and "we don't have a yard," she said. "You have a yard. I feel bad for dogs that are cooped up inside all the time. You need to keep Rex here. It's perfect for both of us: Rex gets a yard and I get to see him whenever I want to."

I told her that maybe since she loved him so much, she could come over and feed him and bathe him and play fetch with him and take him for walks. She wished she could, but she just didn't have the time. "Plus," she said, "I don't like walking around in your neighborhood. It's scary. There are too many slow-driving cars. I always think someone is going to jump out and grab me, or shoot me, or ask for directions." She had an excuse for everything. Here's what she was basically saying: I just want to come over to your house and play with him. I don't ever want him to live with me, and I want none of the responsibility of taking care of him. I want you to be responsible for his well-being, and you can never get rid of him.

You might be thinking, what was the big deal? The big deal was this: dogs are a serious pain in the ass and— this is the most important part—I hate dogs. I've always hated dogs. They're stupid. They're slobbery. They're too friendly: they jump on you and bring you sticks and chewed up, slobbery odd things, as gifts, as things for you to throw and for them to retrieve and bring back. Dogs bark. And howl. This dog, the one with whom I was stuck, was big, so when it jumped on you once, you had to go change your clothes and maybe take a shower. I don't know what kind of dog he was, but Rachel said he was a Labrador mix of some kind. It didn't matter to me. I hated him.

We found him at the dump, on our last trip of the day. I'd moved into a new house and the previous tenants had left behind all this junk. They had seriously trashed the place. We had to haul out all the trash and take it to the dump. That was part of the deal. That was why the rent was so cheap.

We had finished unloading my friend Greg's truck, and I was sweeping out the bed when up walks this dejected thing. I picked up a dead D battery from the bed of the truck and threw it at the horrible creature and yelled, "Git!"

What are you doing? says Rachel. Poor thing, she says. We gotta do something. She looks at Greg. We gotta do something, right? Greg shrugs his shoulders and looks at me. I'm finishing sweeping and pretending I'm not listening. Okay, I say, let's go. No, she says, we can't leave. Look at it. You can see its ribs. It's starving. No, I say. This is a dump. There is plenty of food here. There is food everywhere. You can see its ribs, sure, but that's only because that's the way the dog is supposed to look. That's a trait of the breed. (I, of course, know nothing of dog breeds or their traits.) Greg says, no, you can't dump food waste here. There's nothing here for him to eat. It's not that kind of dump. I glance a shut-your-face at Greg. Look, I say, it'll be fine. He probably eats raccoons and rats and opossums. It's a dog, for Christ's sake. It can hunt. She walks toward it and it walks toward her. God, I say. This is disgusting. How do you know it doesn't have rabies, or heartworms? You know it has fleas. I guess it can ride in the back, says Greg. I give Greg another look. Are you going to take him? I say. No, he says. I can't. My wife hates dogs. Plus, he says, we've got too many animals as it is. We're taking him, says Rachel. He can stay at *your* house. Your new house. It has a fenced in yard and everything. It's perfect.

Six months went by and, believe me, things happened. It's really quite complicated and I did some things that I'm not proud of. I did things that have changed everything. I made some bad choices.

I knew right away that I couldn't take him to a shelter. There's only one in the tri-city area and Rachel's best friend, Tracy, worked there at the time, and you don't even want to know how much of a pain in the ass she was. Whenever there was some kind of dispute, anything, she automatically sided with Rachel, no matter what. About three years before all this, for instance, Rachel did something inexcusable. She cheated on me. Not once, either. Three times. With three different guys. Within a month's time. I was devastated, naturally. We kind of broke up for a couple months. But we ended up, obviously, getting back together. Rachel apologized, and I forgave her because, I thought, I was lucky to have her. But a few weeks later, I was standing outside of Rachel's front door and Tracy was inside with Rachel and they were talking, and I overheard Tracy say that the whole thing had been "Richard's fault to begin with. It never would have happened if he'd been more of a man." I couldn't believe it. What did that even mean? What did it mean to be a man? And how was she, Tracy, any kind of expert on the subject? I'd never even seen her with one.

Four months after I got him, I took him to this neighborhood called Spring Haven on the other side of town. It was really uncomfortable for me because I'd never had him in my car before, and I could feel its value plummeting. Not that it was a great car. It was a piece. But dogs stink and I knew that my car would never smell right again. Anyway, I took him to Spring Haven and I left him there, on some anonymous looking street, deep in a vast, sprawling subdivision. On the way back, I stopped at Bruno Burger and had a strawberry shake, and I stopped at a music store and bought a CD. I was feeling normal again. I felt good, and bad. When I pulled into my driveway an hour and a half later, there he was. I'm not shitting you. He just stood there, panting, like he'd ran the whole way, with a meek, dejected look in his big brown eyes.

About three weeks later I saw that Documentary. I think it was called *CATatonia: A Midwestern CATastrophe.* Aside from making me feel ill, it made me think about what I'd tried to do to him. How I tried to leave him in Spring Haven. It made me think harder. I needed to be more creative. What could I do to get rid of this poor creature, something that would cause neither of us any harm? Something that would provide him with a new home and would allow me to keep my girlfriend. No suffering. I hated him, but I didn't want to be unduly cruel to him. I didn't want to be like Deek and his friends, the Little Deeks. And I didn't want him to cause me to lose my woman. But then I thought about Deek's girlfriend. She didn't care what he did, as long as he bought her pretty things. This added a new dimension, possibly. I thought about Tracy at the animal shelter. I thought about Deek's black-toothed adolescent girlfriend kissing her cubit zirconium speck. I thought about how long Rachel and I'd been together. And I thought about how there is one thing that a man can do that will *always* bring women together in his favor.

The ATM would only let me take out three hundred and sixty dollars at a time, so I had to use it three times in a row, incurring a total of six dollars in transaction fees. I counted it: 1,080 dollars. Seeing the money made me second-guess myself. Was this going to work? If it did work, did I accept the consequences? I felt like it would, and I felt like I did.

"Seven. I'm pretty sure it's seven," I said.

The sales associate handed me the plush clamshell with the ring in it and I looked at it and I liked it. "Is this one a seven, or will you need to size it? I'm kind of pressed for time, so if it's not—"

"No. Thees wan ees se*von*," he assured me. I could tell I was boring him to death.

They, all the people in the jewelry store, were impressed by my paying in cash. I acted very nonchalant, like it was nothing for me to be spending a thousand bucks in one fell swoop. But I didn't feel nonchalant. I kind of felt like an ass for letting things get this out of hand, which was a bad sign, obviously, but I ignored it. After leaving the jewelry store I rushed straight home and put him back in my car. One more ride for us.

It was two o'clock and the shelter closed at five so I had plenty of time. In my head I nervously went over the scenario. *Walk in with him on leash. Go straight to front counter. If Tracy is not there ask for her. If Tracy is there say hi, and show her. Nothing about him. She will most likely say wow it's beautiful! Is it for her? Yes. Doing it tonight? Yes. She will say wow again. Very casually, coolly, bring up the dog. She will understand. After all that she'll understand. Won't even have to explain. It's all there. There's no explaining something like that. People just understand. She'll take him and smile. Good luck, she'll say. Easy. Over.*

We walked through the front door and there she was, hunched over the front counter, writing.

"Hey."

"Hey. What are you doing here?"

Being a man. Doing the manly thing. "I've got something I need to show you, Tracy. I need to know what you think, I need your advice." It was smooth to throw in the I-need-your-advice bit.

"Oh, yeah," she said. "It better not be what I think it is, though." She looked at me sideways and then looked at the dog.

"Well," I said, a little worried now. What could she mean? I hoped she wasn't referring to him. "What do you think *it* is?"

"Never mind, Dick." I forgot to mention. She liked to call me "Dick." She got a kick out of it. It was a small form of verbal abuse that she delighted in. "What is it?"

I pulled out the box and sat it on the counter, and pointed to it. She picked it up and held it about breast-high and looked at me, as if to say "really?" and then she opened it. I smiled because, so far, my plan seemed to be working.

"Diiick," she said. "I don't know what to say. I didn't even realize we were friends. Well, I'll have to think it over, of course."

"Shut up. Quit playing. Do you think she'll like it?"

"Yeah. She will. It's beautiful. I wouldn't have thought you had such good taste."

"Thanks, sort of." Now for the tricky part. If things were going to unravel, this was where it would happen: "Anyway. One more thing. With things being the way they are…now, I'm going to have to get rid of him…Rex." (I was so committed, I actually said his name.) "I obviously can't keep him around anymore. So that's why I brought him—"

"Wait a minute. You're trying to bring Rex to *my* shelter? You know how much she loves that dog." She leaned against the counter, and her breasts were sitting on it like two large loaves of bread, and her head and angry looking eyes were about a foot away from my face. I could smell her breath: onions.

"Yeah, I know, but if things are going to happen then things will have to change. We can't have this dog around, stinking everything up." I was losing some ground here. I could feel it.

"What are you talking about? Rachel loves that fucking dog. Frankly, I'd be surprised if she didn't want it to be the ring bearer, or the flower girl. Look, you're crazy if you think you're going to unload it on me. You're not dragging me into this sick shit."

"Sick shit! I just want to get rid of this dog. That's all. I don't want him. I hate him. Why can't I make a decision to get rid of him? Why can't that be okay? He's *my* dog for Christ's sake! Why can't I get rid of my dog? Why do I have to sneak around and lie and make shit up and do morally reprehensible things, like drop him off in other towns." I stopped and gripped the side of the counter so hard the skin under my fingernails turned white. "I hate this dog, and it's making me a bad person!"

Something happened to me there in the animal shelter. The plan had unraveled. I had unraveled. Things had happened.

"You *are* screwed up, man," said Tracy. "You and Rex need to leave. You're making a scene." She turned and walked away.

Back home, I wondered. How had all this happened? A total lapse in Judgment. Desperation. Sneakiness. Dishonesty. Tracy was right. I was not a man. To be truthful, I didn't know what it meant to be a man. Sitting in my chair, staring at the ring, cozy in its little velvety box on the ottoman, I knew that I didn't know what it meant to be a man. Poor stupid dog, I thought. It was outside on the front porch. A storm was approaching and I knew he would soon begin howling, and I knew that I needed to quit lying to myself. It was time to be honest, to sort out the truths from the lies.

These were the only truths I knew: I hated him. And I hated her.

It was the first time I ever allowed myself to think it. I'd felt it before, but I had never let myself think it. It was the first time I truly knew it. It wasn't love that kept us together. It was fear. I was scared of being alone, and she was scared of being with someone who wasn't scared.

I let myself say the words: "I hate her." They sounded tentative, of course, like I'd just learned them, but it felt good.

But what did this mean? I had no idea, but I felt oddly good. I felt unburdened. I heard thunder, but I did not hear him. I sat there, silent. More thunder. More silence. I got up and walked to the back door and opened it and there he was, curled up in a comfortable looking nap position. I nudged him on the back with my foot. He didn't move. Not a twitch. It was raining hard. There was lots of thunder. Loud. Close lightning. I reached down and touched him. He felt warm. He felt soft. I tried to rouse him. No movement. Sideways rain hit us. I looked around. A car was coming. Rachel's car. Rachel. I bent over and picked him up. I held him to my chest. I'd never held him before. He was not heavy. Rachel's car pulled into the driveway. Its headlights shined on us. The headlights did not go out. I kept waiting for the headlights to go out, but they didn't. They kept shining as I stood there, wet, on the porch, holding a dead dog I hated, and waiting for a woman I hated to turn off the lights and come toward me, through the rain.

Unmentionables

After the accident, it had taken a year for Rick and Linda's marriage to completely dissolve. With Sarah's death went the one mooring of their union, and they drifted further and further apart until they completely lost sight of each other. Part of the problem was that the accident hadn't been anyone's fault. Black ice in the middle of the night. Rick had been driving, so he felt at fault, and beat himself up about it for a while, but there was no evil to point to, no monstrosity to blame, to hate, so they were just angry with themselves, with each other. Eventually, Linda moved in with her sister, Susan, but she disappeared after a few weeks. She took almost nothing with her. Just walked out one day, leaving behind a note that said, "Don't look for me. Linda." After three months, no one expected her to return. Rick worried about her, but he understood. She'd lost her child, and that loss hollowed out everything else. He felt like he belonged nowhere. Finally, he followed Linda's example and took to roaming.

They sat and drank their beers and smoked quietly, like two old friends, though they'd only known each other for a few months. Reese picked up the remote and flipped through the channels and stopped on a soccer game, Wales versus Scotland. Rick had stumbled into a job washing dishes at a tacky fried-fish joint for tourists, folks who didn't know any better. It also happened to have drag shows after midnight. The Golden Dolphin, it was called. Reese was a server there, by day, and a performer by night.

"I didn't know you were a soccer fan," said Rick.

"I like the little shorts they wear," said Reese. He winked and opened what looked like a pink tacklebox.

"Jesus," said Rick. He grabbed the remote off the coffee table and changed the channel.

"You brought it up, dear." Reese was applying a base coat of make-up to her big, manly face.

"You never said what you're getting all gussied up for?"

Reese put the tiny baton back in the pink box. "Well, I'm glad you asked. I need an escort. Interested?"

"Where to?"

"Maxine's. You know Maxine."

"She's the other brunette in the show."

"That's right. Patty is the little blond. Anyway, Maxine is having a costume party at her place, and she's invited everyone from the Dolphin. Your boyfriend Joe might be there." Joe was a straight guy who frequented the drag shows. He found it all amusing. For him, there was nothing sexual tied up in any of it. He just got a kick out of seeing men dress up as women and parade around lip-syncing on a stage. He could often be found leaning against the bar smiling. He disrespected any of the performers, so no one ever kicked him out.

"Cute. Isn't that sexism or something?"

"Whatever. You up for it?"

"I guess."

"Of course, we'll have to find you a suitable dress to wear."

"Sorry?"

"Well, it's an all drag party. There'll be queens from as far as Sahwoklee County. If you go, you *must* go in drag."

Rick protested for about an hour, but as he became progressively drunker he began to warm to the idea. He thought it might be amusing. He wasn't inclined *that way*, but at this point, he figured he'd try anything once.

They went into Reese's bedroom and looked for something for Rick to wear. Rick was tall, like Reese, but much thinner.

"How about this, bruiser?" Reese held up a black-and-white polka dot dress. "Fifteen years ago this was my favorite. Joan Crawford. You should have seen me back then." She made a show of sucking her gut in.

Rick noticed the dress was hung on a wire hanger. He pointed it out to Reese but she was not amused.

"Focus, Ricky, focus." She hung the dress back on the rack and lightly touched a few others as if she were not only considering options for Rick but also remembering times she'd worn each one. She sighed and looked back at Rick.

"Well, you're thin enough. We can really make you look fabulous. We could make you look stunning. Do you want to *be* stunning?"

"Well, I guess I don't want to look like total shit, if I can help it."

"I think we can manage that."

Looking at all the dresses and shoes and wigs and scarves in the closet, Rick realized that Reese had more women's clothes than he had clothes period. Reese, he thought, was living two lives, had to have the belongings of two people. He looked around at the clothes-cluttered room. Reese's was a full life. The fullness of his own life, he thought, could be measured in fractions. Half a life? Maybe not even that.

"Well, since you're leaving it up to me," said Reese, "I think we'll go for a Garbo look."

"Whatever." Rick tamped out his cigarette in a green and brown ashtray shaped like a palm tree on a tallboy dresser next to the closet door.

Reese handed Rick the dress. "Go ahead with this and I'll pick you out some shoes and a hat."

"A hat?"

"All the women of that era wore wonderful hats. I'll try to find something Anna-Christie-ish."

Rick looked at himself in the bathroom mirror. The black dress went down to just above his knees and his bushy-haired legs looked all wrong sticking out, slightly bowed, his feet still in white crew socks. He took the socks off and looked again. Better. His arms looked good, he thought. The straps of the dress, tight around his shoulders, emphasized his biceps and shoulder muscles. He looked at his face in the mirror.

"You look pretty good," he said to himself.

Rick walked back into the bedroom.

"Turn around," said Reese.

Rick turned.

"Your ass looks great."

"Easy, now."

"Sorry. I didn't mean anything. You're gonna look fantastic."

Reese handed Rick a pair of flat-heeled mules with a splash of sequins on each toe.

"I won't make you wear heels, dear. It's hard enough when you are sober and know how to walk in them. I don't want you to hurt yourself."

Rick put the shoes on and walked in a circle. They were comfortable.

"I can wear these."

"We'll forgo the hat and just part your hair to the side and pin it. We'll use a little product to keep it in place."

Rick let Reese do his hair and watched in the mirror. He was surprised by how unbothered he felt by all this. He also looked better than he'd thought he would.

Reese rubbed his finger over a scar on Rick's scalp. "What's this?"

"Car accident."

"Was it a bad one, or just one of those fender benders?"

"It was very bad. It was another life ago."

"How many lives have you had?"

"Enough."

When Reese was done, Rick stood up and looked at himself in the mirror on Reese's bedroom walls.

"Not bad, huh?" said Reese.

Rick didn't say anything.

"Here," said Reese. She handed Rick a small thin-strapped purse. "For your unmentionables."

Rick took it and put the strap over his shoulder. "I don't have any *unmentionables*."

"Yes you do. Everyone has unmentionables, especially ladies."

"I'm not a lady, remember? Neither are you."

Reese put her hand up to her mouth as if Rick had said something scandalous.

"One last thing," said Reese.

"Really?" Rick looked himself up and down. "What else could there possibly be?"

"We need to put your face on."

After years of turning her own fat face into something feminine and not altogether unattractive Reese had become an expert at cutting the female out of a male face, like a sculptor almost. Seeing Rick made up, one now realized his face had some natural femininity of its own—a somewhat small and pointed chin, large eyes—which Reese expertly emphasized.

"I look like my sister." Rick stood in front of the mirror.

"You have a sister? I never knew. I'd love to meet her."

"I don't *have* a sister. But if I did, I bet this is what she'd look like."

"Well, that's the point, dear. And you look great—except for those hairy legs."

"I'm not shaving them."

"No, I didn't think you would. We can fix that with some stockings."

The ocean breeze swept up over the sea-oat-covered dunes and blew against Rick and Reese as they got out of Rick's car and walked up the driveway toward Maxine's front door.

Maxine, a tall drag queen wearing a barrel, with apparently nothing underneath it, and a bright-orange bouffant wig, answered the door. Her face was covered in heavy make-up and she looked to Rick like a rodeo clown. She gasped and stood with the door open.

"Darlings! Reese, who is this?"

"You can't tell?"

"Wait. Rick?"

"Yep." After speaking Rick became painfully aware of his completely flat, low male voice. It was something, unlike his body, that he could not disguise. He did not have the same capacity for flamboyance and flair that these men had.

"I had no idea you cleaned up so well. Come in, come in." Maxine moved to the side, barrel thudding against the door as she turned, and Rick and Reese walked in.

"Have a seat. I'll be back momentarily with some cocktails."

Rick sat down on a couch where a very fat, very still drag queen was also sitting. He looked at her and tried to figure out her outfit. She was holding what looked like a microphone and had on a black business suit, black heels, and a short black wig. She looked vaguely like someone.

"You supposed to be somebody?"

"Guess."

"I don't know. I have no idea."

She held the microphone in front of her own mouth. "Rikki Lake."

"Who?"

"Never mind." She went back to being very still. She reminded Rick of those animatronics you see at places like Disney World and Chuck E. Cheese's.

Maxine came back with cans of beer for everyone. "I'm going to be standing all night in this get-up. But I couldn't resist. The old drugstore on fifth street, in Poseidon Beach. They have these great postcards. I always look through them when I go there—I send postcards to everyone, Rick. I'll have to get your address later. Anyway, they had this one—I bought it—it's around here somewhere—of this cute young gal standing on the beach wearing nothing but a barrel, and so, TA-DA!!! That's how I got the idea for this."

Reese suggested going out to the back patio and they all got up and walked toward the back of the house.

A rush of ocean air met them all as Maxine opened the door. It smelled fishy and salty. Everyone stood holding onto their wigs until they sensed they weren't going to fly away with the wind.

"I just can't get over you, Rick. What a transformation." Maxine looked at Reese. "You really have gotten good at turning boys into girls!"

"Well, Rick gave me something to work with, unlike

some people."   Reese looked over at the Rikki Lake impersonator. She was transfixed, motionless again, staring in the direction of the beach. You could hear the waves breaking, but it was too dark to see them. For a time, they all sat quietly and listened.

By eight o'clock Rick was fairly buzzed and there were maybe twenty-five drag queens milling around on the back patio now, screeching, moaning, howling, laughing and giggling. "It's amazing," Rick said to Reese, "what a few beers, a dress, and a whole lot of make-up will do to a full-grown man."

Reese hadn't left Rick's side the whole time. She was being protective. Rick appreciated it. No matter how many nights he'd spent at the Dolphin, or at Reese's apartment, surrounded by these very same people, he wasn't quite prepared for this. He trusted them, and many were firends. But this night, for reasons he couldn't quite articulate, was different. He was dressed like one of them, and that somehow changed things.

"Well, that's where you're wrong."   Reese sipped from a can of Schlitz.

"How's that?"   Rick held the hem of his dress between his index finger and thumb. It felt soft, like velvet.

"These people were never 'full-grown' anything. I'm not a 'full-grown' anything. Who is?   It's a lie, full-grown. Adulthood. Being a man or a woman. It's all a kind of story people tell themselves." He looked intently at Rick. "I'd like to know what kind of stories you tell yourself."

Rick didn't respond. What Reese said sounded right. These men were more like children, or some of them, even babies. He thought of the one dressed like Rikki Lake, holding onto her microphone, like a baby's rattle, barely saying a word. A large, obese infant.

"We're all something stunted," Rick finally said.

"Oh, so morose," said Reese. "You always glom onto the sad parts of things. We're at a party. Let's behave like it!"

Reese stood up and said she'd be back in a few minutes and then she danced off into the house.

Reese sat and watched everything going on around him. He was feeling more comfortable now. At times he even forgot he was wearing a dress, make-up, stockings, or that he had a small purse for his *unmentionables* slung over his shoulder. In fact, he thought, this doesn't feel that out of place at all. Every time he crossed his legs he felt his thighs touch together through the stockings he wore. It wasn't anything like wearing pants. It was more like being naked. It was a freeing feeling, which was odd, considering he'd always heard that women's clothing was *less* freeing and more restrictive than men's clothing. It didn't seem that way to him now.

He felt an urge to be completely naked. He looked out toward the beach and the waves he could only hear and he pictured himself running naked into the water. He laughed at himself and went to stand up but realized he had an erection. He stayed seated and covered himself with the handbag. For my *unmentionables*, he thought. He closed his eyes.

Rick opened his eyes and looked around and there was no one on the back patio with him. It was very quiet. He sat and listened to the undulating swoosh of the waves and let himself wake up. He stood up and took a few steps toward the end of the patio and he heard a voice from inside the house say, "Oh my God! What *is* that?" And then there was a chorus of prissy screams followed by hysterical laughter. "Oh, don't be coy," another voice said. "You know, you know!" More laughter and screams. Rick walked over to a window and looked in. He saw a crowd of bodies, but couldn't see anything else. He looked down the patio deck and saw another window on the far end. He walked over to the window and looked in. It was a different angle, but he still only saw bodies standing around. Occasionally bodies would part momentarily and he'd catch a glimpse of something dark colored, but bodies would shift again and he'd lose sight of whatever it was. For some reason the word "contraption" popped into his head.

They all started dancing in place and shouting. They were all swaying back and forth. But he couldn't quite make out the music. And then they all started clapping in unison. He walked to the back door and tried to turn the knob but the door was locked. "Do I really want to see what they're doing in there?" He decided to walk around to the front of the house and try the front door.

The front door was locked too. "Goddamn it!" he threw his purse down on the ground. He heard a voice from behind him.

"Ma'am!"

He turned and saw a small car on the road in front of the driveway.

"Shit!" He looked down at himself, at his clothes. He picked up the purse and slung it over his shoulder.

The voice called out again. "Ma'am! Vee are lowst. Ken you help?"

Rick squinted to see the man in the car. He was a small-looking middle-aged man, sitting in the passenger seat with his right arm hung out the window. A chubby woman with short curly hair was in the driver's seat. They looked harmless enough.

Rick walked toward the car. It was hard to see the ground, so he walked slowly.

"You say you're lost?" He stood a few feet away from the car. He held onto the strap of his purse in front of him with both hands.

"Yes. Vee are lewking for da KOA kemp facilities. Do you know vere is it?"

A small camper trailer was attached to the back of the car, the kind with a pop-up top. Rick moved closer to the car.

"Uh, yeah," he said. "I can tell you where that is. It's not far from here." He put his right arm on the car door and leaned closer to the window.

He noticed a little girl curled up in the back seat, sleeping. He thought she was about five-years-old. When the man saw that Rick was looking at her, he turned and looked too.

"Granddaughter. Isabelle." The man smiled and looked

at her for a moment. The woman hit the man in the arm with a rolled up road map and said something that sounded like "hike!" and the man turned back to Rick.

"Yes," said the man. "Please. Help us."

Rick explained as best he could how to get to the KOA, and as he did, the little girl in the backseat of the small car roused and pushed herself up into a sitting position. She reached down into the darkness of the floorboard and pulled out a little fluffy lamb and held it close to her. When Rick was done he smiled at the little girl and said hi to her. She just stared at him and held her lamb. The man was looking at Rick's arm now. Rick looked down at his arm too. It was hairy and muscular, a man's arm. Rick looked back at the man.

"Okay. Be safe. Hope you find it all right." He backed away from the window and gave a quick wave of his hand.

"Uh, yes," said the man. He turned to his wife and pointed forward and said something in another language, and the car pulled slowly forward. Rick stood and watched. The car plodded along for a couple blocks. Rick listened to the rocks and sand being crushed under the car's tires. The car finally turned right and disappeared.

A voice came from the direction of the house and Rick turned around. Reese stood at the front door. "What are you doing, Rick? Come inside! It's getting very chilly out!"

Rick hesitated at the end of the driveway. Reese was right. It was quite chilly now.

"Rick!" shouted Reese, again. "Already being solicited for sexual favors, I see. You little tramp!"

"They were lost!" Rick shouted back.

"A chronic condition!" said Reese.

Rick walked up the driveway toward Reese, who was standing at the front door smiling, holding two cans of beer.

"Are you ready to go? We can go if you want. I don't Want you feeling weird."

"Nah," said Rick, "I'm good."

Reese handed Rick a beer and they walked back inside.

Only a few people were in the living room now. Most everyone else was back out on the back porch. Two people were passed out on the couch and Ricki Lake was sitting in a recliner chair asleep, snoring. Rick walked to the bar and sat on a barstool. Reese sat on a stool too. She sighed and started fishing around in her purse. Rick noticed that a Dusty Springfield song was playing on the stereo. Reese pulled a tube of lip balm from her purse and applied some to her lips.

"I had a little daughter once," said Rick.

Reese paused then deposited the lip balm back in her purse.

"In one of your past lives?" she said.

"My only one," said Rick.

Rikki Lake made an abrupt nasal sound and turned in the recliner chair. Her microphone hit the floor.

"And a wife. Still have a wife, actually. Somewhere."

"I'm sorry," said Reese. "Whatever happened, I'm sorry. If you ever—" she stopped. She looked like she might cry. "—want to talk about it or anything."

"I think I scared those poor folks out there. They were looking for the KOA."

Reese did not respond.

Rick looked around the room. It was quiet and peaceful. He could hear the chattering voices of the rest of the party out back on the porch. "I might do that some time," said Rick. "You know. Talk about it. But right now," he stuck out his arms and looked down at himself, "I'm just not dressed for it."

The Patron Saint of Birds

Patricia, my first wife, and I were married five years, but I believe she knew from day one it wasn't going to work out. Prescient, she knew things before they happened—or claimed to—and I tended to trust her premonitions. She understood that you could call a thing into being by saying it. We got married because she wanted to be married for a while—and so did I.

She sat next to me in Mrs. Poole's ninth-grade Algebra class. Mrs. Poole always chewed gum and if she got mad she wouldn't say shit, she'd just chew her gum at you. Real fast you'd quit whatever you were doing that pissed her off. I don't think Patricia ever did any of her homework or paid much attention in class, but she always got A's on her tests. I sucked at Algebra, no matter how hard I tried, and two weeks into the second semester they dropped me down to Consumer Math, or as Coach Striplin called it, Knucklehead Math.

One autumn night, when we were seniors in high school, at a party in a deep hollow out in the north woods, Patricia said to me, "You gonna ask me to marry you someday, Whitfield Abraham Moody." It was cold and we leaned together against my pickup truck. She'd used my whole name, like she was casting a spell on me. I laughed it off, but that summer after graduation I was drafted into the Army and I didn't cotton to the idea of shipping out to Vietnam without having someone to pine over me while I was gone.

I took off work early one Friday, took my old .22 long shot, my squirrel-hunting rifle, to Brigg's Pawn. They had a simple 14 karat gold ring there and Brigg took my rifle and twenty dollars for it.

Patricia worked at a plant nursery and I walked her into the orchid house, aquamarine and dank smelling, and got down on one knee and looked up at her, a finger of topsoil smeared across her right cheek like warpaint. She said, yes. I'll never forget this: she never said, I told you you'd ask me to marry you. I expected her to, but she never did. In the end I expected many things of her that she never did, and I reckon I did too many things she had not expected. We did not erupt, we did not fight, but when I rotated back stateside after my tour in Vietnam, we drifted away from each other, slow at first, then fast.

The mind is like a bird, I think, as I sit here on my front porch and watch the swallow-tailed kite do its thing, as I have done in these months since my retirement. It flies high, in figure eights, and damn if it don't look just like a child's kite. I've never been one for reminiscing or for being nostalgic, or for regrets, for that matter, but I imagine we all have moments in our pasts that our minds will light on, from time to time, birdlike, without our even thinking about it. Touchstones of memory, you might say. I'm old and I watch birds. But don't call me a birdwatcher. I worked on semis all my life, but I never once, that I can recall, referred to myself as a diesel mechanic, unless I was filling out tax forms. The swallow-tailed kite, I've decided, is a gorgeous bird— gorgeous in a sneaky way, like some women.

Susan was unexpected. Patricia had worked a kind of spell on me—had put roots on me—but Susan was guileless and possessed a raw, natural beauty. I met Susan at a diner in Charleston, three years after Patricia and I had divorced. I ordered a coffee—cream and sugar—and a cup of cheese grits and she took my order and brung them to me. I sat down at my tiny table by the window and she walked over and stood next to me without saying a word.

She pulled a pen and pad out of her apron pocket, clicked the pen several times, and stood waiting for me to order. I said, "Excuse me..." and she put her large brown eyes on me, but she did not utter a word. I ordered, transfixed by her expressive eyes that seemed to be reading me, and she slowly wondered off, as if her walking had no purpose. She did her job well, easily, but she seemed too blasé about it. She lacked a waitress's sense of urgency. After she put my food down, she went over behind the register and stood there, and talked to no one and her colleagues seemed to move and break around her, like water around a rock. She just looked around mechanically and kept smoothing her hands across her skirt until a party was sat in her section, then she'd slowly and gracefully wander over.

I worked that day on a 1949 American-LaFrance 700 that the CFD kept around. The fire chief said they didn't really use it but liked to keep it running for parades and special events. It was a beauty. They'd kept it in great shape and working on it was a joy. Compared to more modern trucks, it seemed like there was about four feet of elbow room around the engine. I did the repairs—new plugs and starter, easy stuff that they probably could have done themselves—and spent the rest of the day at the fire station, bullshitting with the crew. They recommended a barbeque place called Rip's, so I went there for dinner.

It was a seat-yourself joint, so I walked into the crowded hull of the place and sat down at a small table in the back. The pit was somewhere behind me and I could smell the woody smoke, sweat and thick. I looked through the menu and was settling on the brisket dinner when I heard a pen click and I looked to my left and there the hell she was. This time she wore a nametag: Susan.

"You look familiar," I said. Two waitressing jobs, I thought, damn.

"Fah-mill-yer?" she said, squinting her eyes at me. Her voice sounded like a fair impression of a human voice, like she'd learned to speak English too quickly and had to figure some of it out on the fly. On this second look at her, I recognized more fully now the careless beauty she possessed.

I told her my order while staring at the mouthwatering pictures on the menu. I'd unexpectedly worked up a raging appetite. Also, we had no good barbeque places in Dunbar, so I was really looking forward to this meal. She tapped me on the shoulder, startling me. I looked up at her and, in her uncertain voice, she said, "Please, tell me your order," then she point at her eyes. "Look at me," she said.

"Oh shit!" I said out loud and she smiled at me and put her finger to her lips.

"I'm sorry," I mouthed and she smiled a little wider.

I ate my meal in awe of her that evening. The whole place sang its cacophonous song around her and she didn't hear a goddamn note of it. I watched her float from table to table, unhurried, like a honeybee, squinting at patrons as they spoke their mute orders to her.

It's hard to believe nowadays, but Susan knew no sign language. Her family, I'd find out, had neglected her, had ignored her, were ashamed, and she had learned to read lips. Her ability was prodigious. She could decipher the most garbled mouthings.

I got hooked on her and found myself taking weekly trips to Charleston, and to her workplaces. I dropped a lot of money on grits and brisket. After a couple months of this we started seeing each other and in six months' time she had quit her jobs and moved into my place in Dunbar.

Nobody back then called it that, but I had PTSD from the war. I was a mess and no matter how hard I tried I was no good for anyone. And I did try. I tried hard. There was, more or less, a pattern. I'd be good for three or four weeks. But I could feel it building, a little at a time, the black void and its awful pressure, like a black hole, as it squeezed out reason and patience and kindness and all the good things inside of me. When the pressure became too much, I'd bust open and the blackness would pour out of me and as it poured out, I poured whiskey on it—poison on poison. I did not break her heart. We hadn't been together long enough, and I had not shown her enough decency in that short time, for her heart to be that full. But I broke my own heart, twice. Once when I hurt her, and again when she left. She did the right thing. I never saw her again and I hope that she went off somewhere and found some of the goodness the world has to offer, because there is so much of it.

A kite is an uncommon creature. It's long and its tail looks, of course, like a swallow's, but much larger, and its wings are long and narrow and suggest an albatross's. The head of a kite is tee-niny, and hardly visible when one is flying high, but when it gets close to the ground, as it rarely does, you can see that it's hawk-like. There are other birds around these parts: sulky crows, tedious mockingbirds, covetous grackles, pathetic doves, proud cardinals and dignified blue jays—and I've seen a frantic hummingbird in the backyard a time or two. Summer nights you can hear a chuck-will's-widow, which is what they got down here in Florida, instead of whip-poop-wills. Chuck-will's-widow is a nightjar, like the whip-poor-will, but its song is slower and more mournful sounding.

After Susan, and after I had hit a pretty hard low, I cleaned up my act and threw myself into work. I worked eighty hours a week most weeks, and I did a lot of traveling for work. I went all over West Virginia, Southern Ohio and East Kentucky. I worked on every kind of truck, but I liked haul trucks. I spend one whole week, in the winter of seventy-six, just outside of Lexington, working on a Titan ultra-class coal hauler, biggest damn thing I'd ever seen, when things took a turn. The foreman of this coal yard was a man named Cedric Helm. Helm had a booming, forceful voice. He was friendly and jovial, but if he thought you were trying to screw him somehow, he'd rip into you lightning fast. He was a rare thing in these parts—a catholic. Cedric was in his fifties and had a sister, Named Edna, who was about my age, and, like her brother, a catholic. Edna, I quickly found out, didn't want you to call her Edna. Louise was her middle name and that's what you'd call her if you wanted her attention. Louise was a fine woman—attractive, smart and independent. And in all this time, she'd never married.

While I was lying under the belly of that Titan one afternoon I heard the gravel crunch and I heard it stop near me and I heard Helm talking to someone whose voice was almost as big as his own, was like an echo of his. The two voices bounced around outside of the cave the undercarriage of the Titan created and I got to where I had to go look. I crawled out from under and the sun cut into my vision and I had to blink several times before I could see anything—but Helm spoke out.

"There he is," I heard him say.

I squinted toward Helm.

"This here's Edna Louise, my little sister."

"Louise will do," she said.

I stuck my hand out in her direction. The sun began to move to the other side of the Titan and our spot slowly darkened. It was like someone rolling up a tinted car window. The temperature seemed to drop ten degrees.

"Call me Whit," I said.

She whispered "Whit" and smiled at me through the shade. She was just dropping by she said. She had to get back to work. She and Helm both turned away from me and slowly walked toward the foreman's trailer where Helm spent most of his time. I worked for another hour and a half on the Titan and the whole time never stopped thinking about Louise.

Once I'd cleaned up I walked over to Helm's trailer, knocked on the door.

"Closing up shop," I said.

"Me too. Hey, come have a cold one or two with me." He closed a binder he'd been looking at and stood up.

I hesitated.

"I'll drive…"

I loaded my tools into my truck and walked over to Helm's and we rode out.

The bar Helm took me to had no name. It was across the street from a butcher shop called Hamilton's, though, so everyone called it Across from Hamilton's or Next to Hamilton's or, sometimes, people would come right out and call it Hamilton's. Helm said that once, many years ago, he'd asked the owner, a grizzled old guy named Rudolph Highmark, why he had never named the place and he said, "A bar don't need a name." That's it. No explanation. But, to my mind, he's right. A bar serves alcohol, and if you're the only one around for miles, people will come to your bar, even if it doesn't have a name—and they'll create a name for it.

Helm got straight to it. "Let me ask you something, Moody. What do you think of my sister? What do you think of Louise?"

I told him I thought she seemed real nice and was an attractive woman.

"She's rich too," he added.

"What's going on here?" I said.

"She said she thought you was handsome and asked about you. Asked if you was available. Said she didn't see no ring."

"I'm used to brothers shooing men away from their sisters, not soliciting callers for them."

"Look. She ain't exactly getting younger, and she's a good woman. She's looking for someone to share things with."

After some back peddling on my part and some begging on his, I told Helm I'd do what he asked. He wanted me to have dinner with him and his sister the next night. I'd be in town and I liked free food and I didn't see any reason not to. Plus, I wasn't lying. She was attractive to me. I couldn't figure out, though, why she wasn't already married with a ten- or twelve-year-old kid.

The dinner went well. She couldn't cook worth a shit, but we hit it off from the start. We shared many common interests. She liked to travel and had an RV and had been all over the place. We swapped tales of our travels. Helm popped the cork on a bottle of red wine I'd brought and once it was empty, Helm left, with a sly smile, and I stayed. Louise opened up another and we went out back. She had a nice wide deck that looked out on an old-growth pine forest that had long ago climbed its way up the side of a mountain. We sat and drank and talked and listened and, when the wine was gone, we went to bed.

She looked into my drunken eyes. "I'm, a lot of the time, disgusted—by the thought of..." She rose and finished undressing. She turned and smiled. "But you don't disgust me."

"You don't disgust me neither," I said.

She got under the covers. "Take all of your clothes off."

I complied and stood there, in the buff, while she looked at me.

"Okay," she said, "you can get in."

I got under the sheet and comforter and lay there, not sure how to proceed. Louise was different.

"Do you mind if we lie here for a while?"

I said I didn't mind. And as I lay there the wine began to work its dark magic and I drifted off.

I converted and Louise and I had a long-as-hell catholic wedding in November, her favorite month in her favorite time of year, and we did not consummate until that night and it was good and we were both happy. We stayed that way for thirty years. Louise contracted pancreatic cancer at the age of sixty-five, in late August, and she was dead by mid-December. That was a year ago.

Sadly, as is always the case, the swallow-tailed kite, reels off and I'm left with the ornery, blathering mockingbirds and the melancholy old doves. These birds are too common to be beautiful or captivating in any real way. But, I wonder, if there were not so many of them, if they were rare, would they be beautiful? They do have a prosaic, plain, simple charm, but that, I'm afraid, is not enough. I only really care about a few catholic saints—Mary, who is more than a saint, and Saint Francis of Asisi. Francis was good and decent and loved everyone and everything and you usually see him depicted with birds around him. Did you know they got patron saints of every damn thing—even dogs? St. Gallus, some Swede from fifteen-hundred years ago, is the patron saint of birds. What animal needs a saint? Possums, maybe. Birds damn sure don't.

PLUS TWO

Counting by Mississippis

Only Clemons can tell you *exactly* what happened, but it all started with his family undergoing a kind of culling. It was the cruelest act of nature I'd ever seen up-close, and completely beyond my grasp at the time, being as I was, in those days, a selfish bastard, which is also part of the story. The core of the matter was this: one of Clemons' family members had died each year, for five years in a row—wife, sister, mother, father, and his own son—until he was down to only the ones he didn't like. Each death was by disease, cancers of some variety; stroke took his son. Pneumonia fell Clemons' tall father.

Clemons clung to his sanity for far longer than most would have.

Drinking, of course, occurred—alcohol abuse on a prodigious level—and anyone who knows anything about that knows that it only serves to deepen depression and further disorient the mind, which is exactly what happened for Clemons. He confided in me one afternoon during a sojourn at our respective mailboxes. He told me he was feeling, to use his word, "unmoored" from reality. He also said something about having only "a tentative grasp" on things.

"You need to find something to do, my friend," I told him. "A hobby or something. You got anything you like to do—other than, you know, what you're doing presently?"

He smiled at me and nodded. If I'd known him better, if I had been a better neighbor, I might have intervened at this time. If I had been more like Old Linda, our across-the-street neighbor, I could have been more help to him. But we weren't much more, really, than mailbox comrades, and I hadn't, at that point, cleared out the space in my stunted life for another human and his immense grief. We'd shared an odd beer together, in my or his yard, while bemoaning chinch bugs and dollar weeds—but that had been the extent of it. Old Linda, though, would eventually help me bring proper bearing to all this. That's part of the story, too.

"Last night," he said, while slapping a short stack of envelopes on his leg, "I got so drunk on Jameson that I blacked out and woke up this morning with a blurred, gauzy vision of myself peeing into a loafer." He lowered his head and brought it back up with a twisted smile. "I got out of bed and walked over to the closet." He pointed to his left, as if a closet might be standing there in the yard. "There on the floor of the closet were two brown loafers, one of which was several tones darker than the other. I didn't dare touch it. Just left it there." He squinted at the sun, "Once you've piss in a shoe," he said more to himself than to me, "you're in uncharted territory."

"That's what I'm talking about," I said. "You need to find something—some activity or task—to do to take your mind off things." I don't know if it was good advice, but I was trying to be neighborly, and it seemed to me like a sensible suggestion.

Later that morning, still drunk, he got into his pickup and drove slowly around the neighborhood. Two days later, he related the following to me:

"I rolled to the intersection and turned left onto Raintree [the main road that cuts a circle through our neighborhood]. I passed that boy named Avery on his BMX and waved at him. The boy showed me his middle finger and called him a *creepy fucker*. In retaliation, I told him he had a girl's name, and the boy threw a rock at my truck, but missed." This, Clemons told me, made him cry uncontrollably.

"I couldn't help it. The mourning tore loose of me," said Clemons. He wanted to pull over but he could not do so without pulling into someone's yard, so he kept driving. Finally he came upon a yard sale and, as he rolled by, he saw what looked like an old bike. He pulled to the side and got out and walked to the neighbor's driveway. It *was* a bike; according to Clemons, "a sweet old Cooper Velocrome" road bike. He haggled briefly with the turd selling it and bought it for fifty bucks. "I'll fix it up and sell it," he thought, "and it will keep me from going crazy." He was taking my advice, he told me. It would be a good distraction, something to stop him from venturing too deeply into *the farther territories* (what he'd come to call his nightly drunken journeys into the *internal oblivion*, wherein he brought out of himself and into the world-at-large staggering and sometimes terrifying incoherencies) some artifact of reality to keep him firmly rooted and present in the external world.

This is what *he* told me, in detail, the last time I spoke with him.

Clemons took the old bike into the garage and put it up on the mechanics' bike stand, tightened it down, and took a step back. Even in this beat-up state, it was a beautiful thing to behold. His first real road bike had been a Cooper Velocrome. Cooper wasn't a great bike manufacturer these days—they'd sold out to Wal-Mart—but back in his day, the early 70s, when this bike was made, they had been a top bike manufacturer, and the Velocrome was a prime example of what an American company could do. It was a gorgeous bike. It had exquisite lines and a distinctly classic, almost Italian, look and feel to it. He knew he was going to enjoy fixing it up.

That night Clemons made empty a bottle of Jameson and woke up the next morning naked on the living room couch hugging a Virginia ham like a pillow. He puked three times while showering and had a dry waffle and a Heineken for breakfast. For half the day he did nothing but lie on his back in bed and stare at the wall. He took a brief nap, maybe thirty minutes, wherein he had horrific murder dreams. He got up and went into the garage and looked at the bike. "Fuck you in your rear derailleur," he said and walked back inside.

At dusk Clemons was finally hungry for an actual meal. He got out of bed and walked to the fridge whose contents consisted of one tallboy can of Heineken, a quarter pound of boloney, and a Virginia ham with crude, reckless bitemarks in it. He took out the beer and sat on the kitchen counter and drank it down. While he drank he thought: "I've got no use for boloney. The ham scares me. Drink this beer and go out into it. Fresh night air and some sensible victuals."

He went to the Italian place up the road from us, about a mile, and set at the bar and ordered a meatball sub and a Peroni. The sub was good. It was the perfect thing. The bartender came over and picked up the vacant plate.

"Seems like the days are coarse and revelatory, but unaccustomed," said Clemons to the bartender.

"What's that, sir?"

"Another Peroni would be amenable," said Clemons. He began to feel as if he could not control what he said. This had happened before. The "unmoored" feeling intensified. "Am I becoming a kind of werewolf?"

The bartender smiled and set the Peroni down in front of Clemons.

"This is the mangle of something reputable and once sincere," said the bartender.

Clemons shuttered, thought, "Oh shit!" and went for the beer, but it would not be taken up. He waved a hand into it and the contents churned like a little whirlpool. The bartender smiled at Clemons. His teeth were perfect—but then his whole face changed. He became birdlike. Owllike, to be precise. The young man softly hooted at him.

"Goddamn," said Clemons. "You got some pretty feathers, boy."

"I was brought up on syncopation and everyday parables. It is the everydayness. It's just like Chekhov said."

He winked a big, glassy owl-eye at Clemons. Then he started to cry.

"Heaven's sake," thought Clemons. "It's happening to other people too. We're all losing our minds. We're all mourners. We're all becoming something. I'm not alone." But he was alone, and he was projecting his insanity, as it were, on others.

It was harrowing and, at times seemed impossible, but Clemons managed to pay the dinner bill. As he was getting up off his barstool the bartender asked him if he was okay, but, to Clemons, it came out as something sinister and threatening—a violent barn-owl screech.

That night he managed not to drink, but he didn't sleep either. He sat in a chair in his garage. Sometimes he stared at the bike on its stand and thought about what he'd do to fix it up. Other times he did nothing and thought nothing and was, as he told me, "the very void itself—a human blackhole."

To balance out his sleepless night of sobriety he drank the entirety of the following day. While the sun was out, he drank. He rationalized this drinking by sprinkling in household chores and yardwork. "At least I'm being productive," he told himself.

Clemons paused in his telling. Took a deep, desperate breath.

"You remember seeing me, around noon yesterdee?" I asked him.

He blinked at me.

"You were standing in the yard, in a pair of plaid boxers. Just standing in the middle of your front yard, kind of in a stance, like you were bracing yourself for a tackle."

I stopped to see if any of this registered.

"Seems like…" he said and then stopped.

"I asked you what you were doing and you said, 'counting by Mississippis.'"

"Jesus," said Clemons in response. "Sorry you had to see that."

"You went inside after that, which I was glad for. Any longer and Old Linda might have noticed and called the police." Old Linda liked looking out her front window at the things that happened on our street. She was a widow. A window widow.

That night, Clemons told me, he had dreams of owls on bicycles. All kinds of owls. Barn Owls, Snowy Owls, Screech Owls, Horned Owls, those little Elf Owls—all with long, muscular legs, doing circles and figure-eights on restored road bikes. Some owls spoke French and one, a particularly boyish owl, flicked him off—gave him the middle *feather*, as it were. Another owl, a brindle wearing a Saxobank jersey, peddled up to him, handed him a check for eight hundred dollars and said, "This here's for your trouble. The man what wrote it is dead. There's always someone dead, and the dead have to pay."

I told Clemons, my neighbor and mailbox acquaintance, that he might consider seeking some help. It was all I had left. What can you do for a man who's seeing obscenity-prone owls on bicycles? This was a mistake. I made a big mistake here. Truth is, I'm an asshole. A selfish asshole.

Today, as I write, it is Sunday. Here's what happened Saturday—yesterday—after Clemons told me about the owls. I hadn't seen Clemons since Wednesday, when he told me about the owl dream, and I was worried. Like I said: to my mind, we weren't the stop-by-for-a-visit type friends, so I was reluctant to knock on his door. Old Linda would wander over every once in a while, though. I'd see her knock, be let in, and not come out of Clemons' for nearly an hour. I often wondered what they did in there because I never heard Clemons do anything but joke about Old Linda, make bawdy comments about her, etc. I wondered, sometimes, did they do it? Were these occasional visits conjugal in nature? They were both about the same age and widowed. Old Linda, I said to myself. Sad, old Linda. Why did we call her that, Clemons and I? She wasn't even that old. Maybe forty-eight. What had been her husband's name, I wondered aloud? Bob seemed right. Bob and Linda. Bob had died of—damn, I didn't even know. Stroke, heart attack….Clemons had gone to the guy's funeral, and I had not. Part of my aforementioned assholishness is that I can't imagine why someone would go to a funeral. You couldn't bully me into going to one. But Clemons had gone to Dead Bob's. Had gone of his own volition. Clemons was not an asshole. I peeked out the living room window and glanced over at Old Linda's place. I had an idea.

Old Linda opens the door and smirks at me. Her whole attitude is lightly bemused, and almost knowing, like she'd been expecting me. I sigh and get into it. I point back towards Clemons' place.

"Linda," I say (almost say Old Linda), "I'm worried about Clemons. He's been struggling lately—you know why—and he ain't been out of the house in three days, since Wednesday." I pause, thinking she might want to interject. She does not.

"Anyway, you and Clemons seem pretty close, so I was hoping you might go over and check on him. He and I don't really visit with one another." Pause, again, and she's still smirking. "What do you think? You mind paying him a quick visit? He and I just weren't friends like that."

"You 'friends like that' with anyone?" she says.

This sort of blindsides me. I notice that Old Linda is still wearing a wedding ring. Bob gave her that. Dead Bob and Old Linda. Old Linder. Dead Borb. Jesus. What a fucking question…

"What're you getting at Linda?" I realize my tone is aggravated. "I just want someone to go check up on Clemons. Can you do that for me—for us—for Clemons?"

"Why can't you do it. It's a fairly simple task: walk over," she points across to his house, "knock on the door. If he answers, feel things out. Does he need help? Does he look okay? Does he need anything, does he want to talk? Sometimes people just need to talk, young man. If he does not answer the door, maybe you might want to call the police, the non-emergency number, of course—not emergency. Unless he's dead over there—then call emergency. Anyway, if you call the non-emergency, tell them of your concerns. Have you already tried calling his home phone? This is not complicated stuff here…"

Sounded complicated to me. Plus, she's talking to me like I'm a goddamn idiot, calling me *young man* and all. This is not going how I'd expected it to.

"I don't have a number for Clemons," I say. It strikes me as odd that I don't have Clemons' phone number. OL condescends her whole body at me—it's like she's hovering over me now.

"Are you even *friends* with Clemons?" she says. "Come in for a second."

I decline her invitation in and stand on her stoop and wait for her to return.

She walks farther into her house, where her kitchen must be. She comes back holding a post-it note, hands it to me. It's Clemons' phone number, she tells me. Give him a call, she says.

"You understand, don't you?" she says, as I'm walking away. "The poor man is being slowly murdered by death. A man—a person—can only take so much of it, of death."

Who knew Old Linda was all business like this? I think. She's got no softness to her. She's all jaggedness and sharp edges. She's a dark and stormy night, all to herself. And she ain't *old*, either. It occurs to me, in this stalled moment, that she's ageless. Timeless. There's something immortal to her. Something Pallas about her. Out of that moment, the truth shoots at me from somewhere, like a stray bullet, not meant for me. Friendly fire. It says: *you have not known death, jackass. Every person—every single person—important to you in life is still living and quite healthy and will not die for many years hence.* This realization, in contrast to Sad Clemons' and Immortal Linda's deep darkness, momentarily knocks the wind out of me.

At the end of Linda's driveway, I turn. There she still stands, at her home's threshold, hands folded in front of her, like a mother awaiting the return of a late child.

I hold the post-it up in the wind.

"Thank you," I say. "I will call and maybe go over."

She's statuesque, silent, and a kind of beautiful.

In my kitchen, I stand next to the phone, Clemons' number in hand, but I do not call. I feel, for some reason, acutely perceptive, and in thrall to it, the perception. I'm locked in. I can do nothing but perceive. I move over to the dining room chair and sit and let it wash over me like a swell on a grey day, and here is what comes, clear as a bell being rung, clear as a baby's cry in a quiet house, clear as a preacher's croon at the pulpit: *until you know death, you cannot fully know love.* And then there's a little addendum or post-script: *also, you are an asshole.*

This lyric whispered across the wind, called up from a pit located just behind me, like a portable crater, brings me to the brink of a tiny, private, welcome madness. I set the post-it on the table and pause, take a deep breath. I lock the front door and walk back out into the dusking day. I count as I walk across the green grass to Clemons' front door. So close, really. Door to door: ten Mississippis.

Wrong Kind of Rain

Bill stood up and pocketed his handkerchief, looked up and watched three turkey buzzards glide low, loose circles directly overhead and, in the distance, high above the lemon grove to his right, he could just make out a small fragile-looking helicopter floating under all the high grey clouds.

The body at his feet, in the shallow ditch, was a dump job. He knew that. He glanced around. "Like a giant laid the poor bastard down in the dirt." He talked as if he were accompanied by an attentive but quiet companion. To his left, on the east side of the ditch, was the small dirt lot, no tire tread marks, with County Road 27 just on the other side of it. West of the ditch, Grant Parson's Meyer lemon grove, row upon row upon row, the size of a small town.

It had been Sugar Burkson, in fact, Parson's reticent chief cultivator, who'd discovered the body just before sunup. He'd called Parson instead of the police and Parson called it in. Earlier in the morning, Bill had asked him, more in passing than to get information, "What you figure, Sugar?" His only comment was "Fuck if I know."

Bill walked back to his truck in the burgeoning morning heat, looked at his watch: seven-thirty. He opened the toolbox in the bed of his truck and pulled a can of Busch Light out of the cooler hidden inside. He listened to the squirrels bark and *squee* in a nearby oak tree. The first few gulps were hard to get down and he almost heaved, but by the time he got to the bottom of the can, there it was: the slow spread of soft golden interior light, and he began to feel right again. He chucked the can, empty but for an ounce or so of swill, in the direction of the squirrels. "Reckon that's Walter Pound's charred corpse?" he said to his phantom partner.

"Ought not to litter, Sheriff," said Deputy Lloyd Barnes as he approached Bill. "It's a five hunnerd dollar fine in Highlands County." He smiled at the sheriff, stopped in front of him. "Little goddamn early for an adult beverage, ain't it?"

Bill's drinking was no secret to anyone, but most people, out of respect, didn't give him any shit about it. Together they walked back to the shallow dip in land between the lot and grove where the body lay. Bill wasn't sure he wanted to tell his deputy what he thought.

Lloyd nudged a black leg with his boot and a crackling sound issued from it.

"Crispy fucker."

"Quit kicking at it, boy."

Barnes glanced around, pulled a can of Copenhagen from his shirt pocket, tapped it three times.

"Right off the bat, I got some ideas."

The sheriff considered saying what he thought but stopped himself. Walter Pound was Lloyd's cousin. They were, in fact, first cousins. Walter's daddy, dead for some time now, had been Lloyd's uncle. If this body was Walter

Pound's, Deputy Barnes would have some opinions on the matter, and Bill wasn't quite ready for that.

"Do tell."

"Even without knowing who this is, I'd start with Evil Dead." Lloyd squinted an eye at the sheriff as he put a pinch of dip into his mouth and tongued it into place. It began to lightly rain, just more than a mist.

Lloyd squatted down and took a closer look. "Who are you?" he whispered.

"Plausible," said Bill. Evil Dead were something of a scapegoat for Lloyd. Still the biker gang had crossed his mind, as well. Of the three in the area, they were the most brutal, and they were responsible for many horrors committed in Durdin. Walter had been mixed up with them. But something told him this had not been done by Evil Dead. This, to his mind, was the result of hate, not business—maybe even deep, familial blood hate, the kind that many of the Pounds and Baggotts had for one another. Things had been quiet between the two families for a while, but relations always soured every few years, and when they did, shit would go down.

Lloyd looked up, the way the sheriff had earlier. The rain had intensified.

"Almost seems like the son of a bitch was dropped out of the fucking sky, don't it? But there's no impact impression anywhere, either." Lloyd spat a brown stream of dip, then wiped his mouth. "What you want me to do? I'd love to go put the fear into some dipshit bikers."

"Just hang tight for the moment." He wanted to ask him if Enid, Walter's wife, still lived in Sahwoklee, two counties over, but didn't want to get Lloyd's mind working. If he asked about Enid, Lloyd would no doubt make the leap to the possibility of the body being Walter's, if he hadn't already. "For now, let's just get out of this rain."

Thirty-five years ago, Walter Pound fell out of a cedar tree on the Durdin Elementary School playground and scraped his elbow. Mrs. Hillman, their kindergarten teacher, an ordinary townswoman, ignorant of backwoods feuds and ways, requested Enid Baggott walk Walter to the school clinic. Enid held his hand the whole way there, waited while the nurse fixed him up, and walked him back. At the age of five, they were barely aware of their own last names, much less any tension between their families, and from that day on, Walter thought often of Enid, despite what he would later realize about their families' extreme dislike for one another. Some sixteen years later, at Lillian and Dill Talbert's wedding, something drew them together, and they stayed tangled up.

As Sheriff Bill Register pulled off the small dirt lot of Parson's lemon grove, he believed, but could not yet prove, he'd found evidence of the grim opening salvo in a new skirmish.

Lloyd decided, upon leaving Parson's grove, that he'd not "hang tight," as the sheriff had told him to do. Instead, he found himself turning onto Firebreak Road, a few miles south on twenty-seven, just outside Durdin city limits, and pulling into the chalky white lot of the Evil Dead Clubhouse. The building had been a VFW, but the bikers bought the building a few years back when the VFW moved to a new location closer to town. Two vehicles sat in the lot: a Harley with a confederate flag fuel tank and a black Ford F-150. The truck was always in the lot. The block building was still white with red trim, but there was a narrow sign over the door that read

EVIL DEAD m.c. est. 1945.
If this is Hell, it's really not that bad." -Duchess of Durdin

Lloyd could smell fire, which reminded him of the charred body in the grove, and he felt a wave of nausea, but forced it down. As he approached the back of the building, he heard voices, and as he turned the corner he saw another motorcycle, an old Triumph, all black and chrome. Just beyond the bike, a smoker and two men standing next to it. Lloyd knew better than to sneak up on these men, so he yelled "Boys!" and waved as he came into view.

"Deputy dog," growled the big one manning the smoker. Doug Crenshaw and Lloyd had grown up together, had even been friends in their early teens. Doug was not a Baggott, but he'd grown up swarmed with them. When Doug had joined up with the Evil Dead he'd tried to recruit Lloyd. But Lloyd was set on prowling through Southeast Asian jungles instead. The second man, a skinny tweaker named Spider, watched, as Lloyd approached.

"Getting an early start," said Lloyd, pointing at the smoker.

"Takes about eight hours, if you do it right. Gives you a reason to start drinking early, too." Doug raised his Budweiser and took a swig. He was a big boy, at least six feet, probably two-fifty, but not as big as Lloyd. The one watching was thin and short but wiry.

"Man, that smell…" Lloyd took a few steps closer. The intensity of the smell was about to put him over the edge but puking in front of these two was not an option.

Doug opened up the lid and dense, blue-grey smoke tumbled up from inside.

"Take a look."

Lloyd stepped into the proximity of the two men and stood next to the smoker, next to the big man, and the spidery one moved in on Lloyd's right.

"Goddamn," said Lloyd.

Doug drank the rest of his beer and hurled the bottle into a metal drum close by. He closed the lid on the smoker and Lloyd stepped back, and so did the twitchy one named Spider.

"Was wanting to ask you," said Lloyd.

"Here it comes," said the big one. "I knowed you weren't paying us a social visit." He looked at his partner.

"It ain't like that."

"It damn sure is like that. It's always like that. Any-damn-thing occurs and you or Bill comes peeping around the corner. What's it this time? A purse-snatching?"

"Fine," said Lloyd. "It is like that. No sense in playing make believe." Lloyd fished out his cannister of Copenhagen, put in a dip, spit off the few grains of tobacco stuck to his bottom lip. Somehow this helped with the nauseating feeling from the smoldering pork butt.

"Y'all villains, big man," he continued. "Something bad happens, I come talk to the bad guys."

The wiry one took a big step inward.

"You better settle the fuck down," said Lloyd, with his right hand out in front of him. The man stopped

Doug smiled and nodded at the other.

"Lloyd Barnes, Vietnam badass!"

The thin one chuckled.

"You might be able to scare teenagers and little old ladies talking like that, but you ain't shit here. We'll knock you on the head and drop your ass in a phosphate mine, bury you in an orange grove, come back and eat some barbeque. Ain't no thing to us."

"Speaking of groves," said Lloyd. "Found a burnt-to-a-husk bastard just north of here in a lemon grove. Just set down in the ditch like god laid him there. You wouldn't by chance know anything about that, would you?"

"Sounds gruesome—but then, being a war vet, you seen all kind a shit, ain't you? Dead babies and whatnot."

Lloyd spit a deep brown gob at Doug's foot.

"Look here," said Lloyd. "You and your methhead pal hear anything you let me know. I'll be back and I'll be expecting a fucking anecdote or two."

No one spoke. Lloyd touched the brim of his hat and turned his back on the two men and walked back to his truck.

Back at the station, Bill called Sahwoklee County Sheriff's Office and talked to deputy Ben Lincoln, acting sheriff. Bill's counterpart in Sahwoklee, Sheriff Frank Newsome, was six-months retired and had not yet been replaced, so the erstwhile deputy had taken over. Lincoln, all knew, would assume the role of sheriff officially once the county commissioners got used to the idea, but that was going to require a brief "mourning" period, as Frank had characterized it to his nephew Ben.

Bill asked Ben about Enid, Walter's wife. Ben confirmed that Enid did, to his knowledge, still life in Sahwoklee County—presumably the small town of Cortez.

"As you know, she reported Walter missing three days ago. But I ain't laid eyes on her drunk ass in a while. No telling where she might be."

"As I know? I don't know shit. You ain't gone looking for Walter?"

"Not actively. Who gives a shit about Walter Pound—other than Enid? And I told your boy Lloyd to tell you about Walter when he called yesterday asking about Bradford's cattle gone missing."

Bill told Ben about the body in the lemon grove and his theory on who it might be.

"Lloyd did tell me about Enid's report," said Bill, lying to save face. "I must have forgot. Old age. Think I should talk to Enid though," he added.

"Have you ever talked to Enid, sheriff? She ain't exactly a sparkling conversationalist. And I'll be honest, she's smart as a snakebite, knows what to say and how to say it and has fun doing it. Likes toying with assholes like us."

Bill told Ben that he had talked to Enid before, several times, and that he knew how to deal with her. When Bill hung up with Ben, he sat in his chair and tried figuring how to move ahead until he felt the heaviness of his fading beer buzz and drifted off.

When Bill woke he had a slight headache but he felt surprisingly rested. It was only ten o'clock. Let's see, he thought. Take about forty-five minutes to get to Cortez. Drive around Sahwoklee for an hour or so, see what I see. Get back by about one or two. He stood up and patted at himself, looking for something to look for. Debbie Creel, his secretary clip-clopped into his office.

"Nice nap, Sheriff?"

He grunted.

"Medical Examiner called. Parson's grove body being examined as we speak."

"Thanks, Deb."

She nodded and stood there watching him look around his office.

"You all right, Bill? I don't like it when you're all quiet like this." Bill was always quiet, and she knew it.

"I'mma ride out to Sahwoklee."

Debbie sighed. "This one's got biker stink all over it, don't you think?"

"It's plausible."

"I'd say a damn sight more than plausible. Who else could have done something like that? Could be Cuban mob—Tampa. Just dropping a body off 'in the boonies' or something."

He smiled and nodded and touched Debbie on the shoulder on his way out.

"You see Lloyd, tell him to radio me, please, will ya, Deb?"

Debbie followed him out to his truck and knocked on his window. Bill rolled it down.

She whispered: "Could be a Pound-and-Baggott thing—that burned up body. That's what you're thinking, Bill. I bet it is, ain't it?"

He winked at her.

"Any thoughts on whose body it is?"

He put the truck in reverse.

"Greedy old bastard," said Debbie and she stepped away from the truck.

As Bill Register pulled onto the road, the fact that Enid had reported Walter missing pressed down on him. This is something, he thought. The distinct possibility of a Pound man found burnt up in a lemon grove. Could be a Baggott that done it, could be someone else. More than a few folks hated Walter enough to want him dead. Even, as Deb stumbled on, Cuban mob and affiliates. Even, as Lloyd had suggested, Evil Dead. It was even possible that Bradford's missing cattle figured into things somehow. Anyone of consequence in the crime world on this whole damn peninsula has had, at some point, a reason to at least want the tar beat out of Walter Pound. Also, may not be that fire was what killed him. The burning could be post-mortem. Could be they burnt him up to cover up evidence. Highly possible. What, he thought, would Lloyd do if this all turns out to be true? What if that is Walter Pound's body?

Back at the station, Lloyd was virtually accosted by Debbie Creel.

"You at Parson's with Bill this morning?" she said as Lloyd sat down at his desk chair. She knew the answer.

"Yes, ma'am." Unlike Bill, Lloyd would tell her all he knew, he usually did, but he also enjoyed stringer her along.

"What you reckon happened to that poor soul, Lloyd?"

"Well. Ms. Debbie, I figure he was burnt up."

"No shit, Lloyd. I mean—who you think it is that done it?"

"Can't say. Evil Dead, likely."

"Interesting," said Debbie.

"Why's that?"

For the same reason as the sheriff, Debbie didn't want to say too much to Lloyd about what she thought, about who she thought the body belonged to. If he'd brought up on his own the possibility, she'd have been more than happy to discuss possible scenarios with him—but she didn't want to be the one to plant the idea in Lloyd's head if it wasn't already in there.

"No—it's just that that makes sense. Any idea who it is—the body?"

"Come on out with it, Debbie. I know your minds working."

She picked up a mug from earlier that morning with about an ounce of cold coffee in it and swirled it once then walked it over to the little stainless-steel sink in the corner and dumped it out and ran some water into it.

"Hell, what do I know, Lloyd. You the one been out there."

He sighed, took off his wide-brimmed deputy's hat and set it on his desk, looked down at his left hand.

"I do know for a fact that Enid reported my piece of shit cousin Walter missing a few days ago. Not ready just yet to mention this to Bill. Maybe he already knows. Maybe he doesn't. But that's family business."

"I'll be damn," said Debbie. She could barely contain her delight at Lloyd's mention of Walter and Enid. "This here—I think you're right, Lloyd. This ain't no bikers done this….How'd you know about Walter? Sheriff didn't say nothing about that."

"He tell you everything he knows, does he?"

She just looked down, then over at the wall.

"I called yesterday and talked to Ben, over in Sahwoklee, about a lead on them Brahmans gone missing and he told me—asked me to relay to Bill that Enid had reported Walter missing. I did not relay that message to Bill."

Debbie nodded.

Lloyd continued: "Walter missing. Burnt-up Walter-sized bastard this morning. Don't take too much intellect to sort out the possibilities, does it?"

"Well, Bill talked to Ben hisself just before he left earlier." Debbie patted at the side of her head. "Whose cattle was that gone missing?"

"Them was Leon Bradford's Brahmans."

Leon Bradford, Debbie knew, was married to a Baggott woman. About fifteen years ago, he and Michaela Baggott, Enid's cousin of some variety, got spliced up on the property Leon had bought a year prior for cattle grazing. It had been a big party, over a hundred people in attendance. A Baggott marrying someone wealthy like Bradford was a big deal. Debbie had been there. Kurt Bignall, the grocer, had asked her to go with him. Debbie did not like Kurt much, but she did like weddings, so she'd accepted Kurt's invitation. She asked herself, would Walter Pound be dumb enough to steal Brahmans from Leon Bradford—and would Leon be bold enough to kill Walter for doing it? Lloyd must have read these thoughts on Debbie's face.

"Debbie, Walter'd be crazy enough to steal Leon's cattle, wouldn't he?"

She told him yes, she thought he would.

Bill pulled into the dirt lot at Fuzzy's, looked around, saw one other vehicle, a white Ford F-150. There was a chained dog lying in the shade off to the left side of the door. He knew the dog but couldn't call its name. The dog raised its head when Bill slammed the truck door, watched him walk all the way up to the entrance. There, again, was a light rain. But, as Bill stopped to look at the sky, he noticed a dark, almost purple shelf cloud to the northeast.

Bill went straight to the bar, whereat he noticed two others sitting, but couldn't make them out until his eyes adjusted to the dark.

"Whiskey and a beer," he said to Roof, the tall half-Indian bartender.

"Right up, Bill," said Roof.

Bill lit a cigarette, glanced to his right, took a drag and said, "Jackpot."

Roof set down Bill's drinks and shifted his eyes over to the two lost souls sitting at the bar to Bill's right, then glanced back at Bill. Next to Bill was a slumped over man in his late fifties or early sixties, a near empty mug in front of him, his fingers curled around it. Next to that man was a very small, prematurely shriveled woman in cutoff denim shorts, a striped tank top and flip flops. Enid Pound. Bill was taken by how quiet it was in the place.

Bill set his cigarette in the ashtray groove, did his shot of whiskey, and fished a dollar bill from his pants pocket, got up and walked over to the jukebox, which was lit up like Vegas, desperate for a few songs. But when he got closer to it, he realized the jukebox was busted up. Big chunks of the jukebox's plastic dome were broken off and there were cracks in it. It was still blinking and flashing, but he paused before putting his money in. He also noticed that to the right of the busted up jukebox was a chair, one leg broke off, leaned up against a post.

"What happened to your jukebox, Roof." He said, putting the dollar back into his pocket.

"There was a fight. Jukebox lost." He chuckled and glanced at Enid, who was also chuckling, but hers was more of a wheeze.

"Does it still work?"

"I gather it don't," said Enid, turning on the bar stool and facing the sheriff. She propped her elbows up and leaned back against the bar.

"Enid Pound—that you?"

"You know damn well it is."

"You're just the woman I was hoping to run into today."

"Sure are popular with sheriffs today," said Roof.

"What's that, Roof?" said Bill.

"Old Frank was just in here about an hour ago," said Enid. "He's retired, but don't act like it. Finding it difficult to enjoy the autumn of his life."

"I bet I know why," said Bill.

"Don't take a rocket surgeon to figure out," said Enid.

"Reckon you and I can have a chat ourselves?"

"My policy on talking to the authorities in a drinking establishment is simple."

"Let me guess: I buy, you talk."

Enid smiled and walked over to Bill, still standing by the dilapidated jukebox, and they both sat down at a nearby table. As they sat, a gust of wind drove rain at the tin roof of the bar, making a loud racket.

"Ooh," said Enid. "I love it when the weather is hostile, don't you, Sheriff?"

The drive to Leon Bradford's ranch from the station was about thirty minutes. Lloyd went over what he would say, what he would ask, what he would look for. Brahmans missing—Walter missing. Two facts with a lot of open air between them. He also knew that Bill would not have approve of this trip to Bradford's. Bill did not approve of "hunches" and "gut feelings." Bill was a hard-facts man, a cautious and thoughtful man. Lloyd respected Bill immensely, but Lloyd had his own ways and they had not yet failed him in a major way so he had no reason to second guess himself.

The double track up to Leon's home on the back of the property was partially canopied and Lloyd found himself driving slowly to savor the dark, cool atmosphere, a scene, he thought, right out of a story about Robin Hood or King Arthur. It was one o'clock now and the sun was high and it was hot and humid, when not under the heavy shade of old-growth. But there was the hint of a storm in the north. He noticed fresh tire tread marks in the dirt and wondered if the Bradford's were even home.

When Lloyd emerged from the cave of trees onto the lawn of Leon's home he was somewhat surprised to find Leon and Michaela outside. Leon stood with his hands on his hips, looking down at something Lloyd could not quite make out, and Michaela was pulling a water hose around the right side of the two-story redbrick home. She eventually was out of his view. Leon didn't so much as glance Lloyd's way until he was out of the truck and walking towards the house.

The thing on the ground in front of Leon turned out to be a dead whitetail doe.

"Jesus," said Lloyd, as he walked up to Leon.

"Damnedest thing."

"Looks fresh."

Leon grunted.

"How is it that you're just coming across it then?"

Leon finally looked over at Lloyd.

"What you doing here, Deputy?"

"Wanted to talk to you about them Brahmans stole."

Leon nodded, pointed behind him.

"Michaela and I just got back from town not ten minutes ago. Left here—shoot—around eight, and I don't recall seeing it here then." He scratched at the crown of his head.

"Looks like it just dropped dead, don't it?" said Lloyd. He knelt down and gently put his hand to its neck.

"What I thought."

Lloyd wondered if a doe could have a heart attack or a massive stroke.

Michaela came back around with her water hose.

"Deputy," she said.

Lloyd and Leon stopped to watch her. Leon smiled at her.

"What you doing lugging that hose all over the yard for?"

"Just watering."

"Leon, you too cheap to have some irrigation put in for your wife?"

"Says she likes the watering. Gives her something to do." Leon turned back to the doe. "You help me pick her up and put her in a wheelbarrow?"

Bill watched Enid take a sip from her new mug of beer and watched her light a slightly bent cigarette she'd pulled from a crumpled soft pack of generic cigarettes.

"Walter's candyass cousin still working for you?" said Enid, blowing a cloud of cheap smoke.

"Lloyd still does, yes. Wouldn't necessarily call him a candyass, though. He ain't the brightest star in the sky, but he's a tough son of a bitch and a loyal officer of the law." Bill wasn't being funny. He meant what he said.

Enid grinned a toothless grin and coughed a quick laugh.

"Okay," she said. "Guess you don't know him like I do."

"Being that he's a Pound and you're a Baggott, I wouldn't think you knew him much at all."

"I am married to his first cousin—and I've heard all the same stories as everyone else in this part of the world, except I've heard the real versions."

"Real versions? You mean your and Walter's versions?"

"The realest versions."

She smeared out her cigarette and skated the mug of beer around in the condensation puddle on the table.

"Speaking of Walter," said Bill.

Enid looked him in the eye, and Bill winked.

"You find out anything about his whereabouts?"

"Not precisely."

"Let me get this right. You're talking to the person who reported him missing to try and find out where he is? That don't make a damn bit of sense, does it?"

"It does if you know what I know."

Enid finished her beer and lit her flattened, bent last cigarette.

Bill held up two fingers and Roof turned around and grabbed two clean mugs.

"Go on, then."

"First I want to ask you a few serious questions. No more of this playing around."

"Who's been playing? You ask, I answer."

"It's just that, if you really want to know where Walter is, you'll want to answer me true. I don't give a good goddamn about Walter. He could fuck right off, as far as I'm concerned. He could trip over and fall off the edge of the Earth, and I wouldn't even spill my drink. And to be honest: whether he's alive or dead or somewhere in between—that don't really matter to me, neither. But it's my job to figure things out. So let's you and me figure this shit right here out."

Enid put out her cigarette and crossed her arms and sat back in her chair.

Bill leaned in, put his elbows on the rickety table.

"Walter do something to severely piss off any of these bikers we got around these parts?"

"You got some paper and something to write with? We'll make a list."

Bill sighed and leaned back. "Anything *lately* or serious and longstanding—anything that might stand out in your mind?"

"He's got some outstanding debt with them Evil Dead pussies. But they like having a little debt on you so they can get you to do shit for them to supposedly 'cancel' that debt, which never actually happens. They scumbags, but they ain't stupid, least not the ones running the show."

"You talk like you know about Walter and his dealings with folks."

"Walter wouldn't make a left turn without I told him ready on the right."

"Got him trained, do you?"

"He's just smart enough to know he's stupid, is all."

"So he consults with you on every little thing then?"

"Every little important thing."

"Then you'll know the answer to this question, I reckon: did Walter steal Leon Bradford's Brahmans?"

Enid smiled.

"I'll answer that question. I'll answer it thoroughly. But first you answer a question for me."

"Fine."

"You think you know what happened to him, where he is?"

Bill figured he was in a good spot here, tactically, and decided that telling her the truth would make her angry, put her right in his hands, get her to talk wide open.

"This morning, in one of Parson's lemon groves, offa twenty-seven, we found a body. A burnt up Walter-sized body."

"But you don't know it's Walter."

"Well, the body ain't exactly…pristine. The body ain't exactly recognizable." Bill looked at his watch. "Matter fact, medical examiner probably just now finishing up with it. I'll make a call, soon as we're done here, and I'll let you know on the spot what they tell me. But, right now, I want to know what you know."

Enid lowered her head and Bill thought she must be crying. Her shoulders jerked a few times. She then held her head up and took a deep breath, looked back at Bill, eyes aglow, brow set.

"Walter did steal that crazy fucker's cattle. Stole the shit out of 'em. But seeing how Walter don't own a fucking tea towel, he had to line up some help. And that help, I reckon, fucked him."

"Go on."

"Walter had the idea of using a couple side-by-sides, corralling as many as they could into a semi-trailer, and hightailing it. In and out. Wee hours. Only Walter, like I said, ain't got shit. So he went to that Evil Dead dick Douglas. He and some other asshole got the side-by-sides and the semi and trailer and they pitched in on the job. Douglas had another 'friend' of his rebrand the cattle and take them to auction. Got top dollar, too. They sold them Brahmans and didn't give Walter a red fucking cent. About two days after that I lost track of Walter."

"So you do think Douglas and his bunch killed Walter."

"You asked me if he stole them Brahmans. I told you he did and told you how they did it. I didn't say word fucking one about who I think killed Walter. But since you brought it up, I'll tell you what I think for free." She paused and glanced to the left. "I need to take a trip to the little girls' room."

"You ain't gonna run off, are ya?"

"What the hell for? But there better be a fresh one on the table when I get back."

"Thought this one was gonna be for free."

"Reconsidered. Nothing worth having is free."

When she returned, Bill offered her one of his cigarettes. She took it, lit it, and took a long pull on the new beer in front of her before beginning.

Bill held up two fingers again and Roof hustled over two more mugs of beer.

"Thing is, you cain't never be too sure with these waterheads we share blood with. Why Walter and I moved out here to Cortez. We still close, but far enough that we ain't having to constantly worry."

Bill and Enid sat and sipped for a while. Bill was perplexed. If Enid was telling the truth, he wasn't sure how to proceed. He lit a cigarette and noticed Enid watching him. He reached his pack across the table and she took another one from the pack.

"Winston's," she said. "Fancy."

He watched her take a match from a folded-up matchbook and slowly drag the match across the ignitor strip. She help up the match and looked at Bill, then lit her borrowed cigarette.

After exhaling a drag that seemed to consume half the cigarette, Enid spoke.

"What about Leon. You go and talk to Leon and Michaela about any of this?"

"What do you mean, what about Leon and Michaela?"

"Leon is a sad bastard—but you cain't imagine the shit Michaela's managed to do without any law finding out. She's small but she's cunning and she's a nasty little bitch. Leon wouldn't hurt a yellow fly but Michaela—being married to Leon is like a mask of respectability. She's shady."

"Sounds ridiculous," said Bill.

She smiled as she smashed her cigarette butt into the ashtray.

"She likes it that you think so."

The deer was not heavy but it was somewhat difficult to pick up and maneuver into the wheelbarrow.

"Got a roll-off around the house," said Leon.

Lloyd followed Leon. They walked by the garage, door open, and Lloyd admired Leon's old caddy, a fifty-nine.

"You'll have to take me for a ride in that beauty one of these days."

"How about today?"

Lloyd did not respond as they were at the roll-off and Leon had set the wheelbarrow down next to it.

"I guess," said Leon, "just take your side and I'll take mine and we'll hoist her up and over."

It was quick work and as they were walking back to the garage to put away the wheelbarrow, Lloyd remembered why he was there.

"Anyway," said Lloyd. "I was meaning to ask you about them Brahmans you had stole last week."

Leon nodded.

Michaela came around the corner, into the garage.

"Y'all done with the 'barrow?"

Leon said yes and she picked up a bag of Black Kow and dropped it into the wheelbarrow with a grunt, then wheeled it off. She was a little younger than Leon, and she was strong for her size, too, which Lloyd guessed to be about five-foot-three.

"Have y'all made any progress on the case?" said Leon.

This question almost startled Lloyd and it took him a few seconds to answer.

"No sir, but I wanted to ask you some questions."

"That'll be fine," said Leon.

"I know you and Michaela ain't ones to get mixed up in all this Pound-Baggott garbage—as you know, I ain't either—but I still wanted to ask you if you was aware of anything that might have passed by me. As far as I know, things have been fairly quiet lately."

"Well, hell," said Leon. "You'd know more than Michaela and me. We're far removed from all that fighting and whatnot."

Lloyd nodded. He was beginning to become aware of a sound behind him, a thumping-whirring sound, that seemed to be coming from all directions.

"That's what I figured, too," said Lloyd. He turned and saw a helicopter coming closer. "I had to ask, though." He had to talk louder, as the helicopter was quite close now. He looked at Leon and Leon grabbed his shoulder and pointed towards the front of the house. Leon's hair was raised up now and he squinted.

They both jogged to the front yard.

"Leon—why's a goddamn helicopter landing in your backyard?"

Leon smiled nervously, his demeanor somewhat changed.

"Michaela has always been fascinated. Always wanted to learn."

"Learn what—to fly a fucking helicopter?"

"Yes, that's right. She's taking lessons."

"From who?"

"That Sugar—Parson's boy."

"Where'd he learn to fly one?"

"Air Force, I reckon."

An idea was beginning to form in Lloyd's mind. It wasn't all joined up yet, but there was enough. He thought about how the body at Parson's lemon grove seemed to have been laid there by magic. And Sugar had allegedly found it.

Keep calm, he told himself.

"Well I think that's great," he said. "Good for her. Man, how's she coming along? I bet it's complicated. I know it's hard to learn."

"Oh, pretty good." Leon's hands were in his pockets now.

"How many lessons she have so far?"

"Not sure, a few."

Bullshit, thought Lloyd. If she were taking lessons, they'd be expensive—he'd know exactly how many she'd taken. Course he might just be nervous. I need time, thought Lloyd.

"Anyway, I wanted to ask you—you got any idea who might have stole your brahmans? Just thought I'd ask. Wasn't sure if anyone had asked yet."

"How the hell should I know, Lloyd? Don't you think I'd have told you something like that, if I had an idea?"

Lloyd could barely hear anything but the helicopter now. He gave Leon a smile and a thumbs up.

They both stood and watched the helicopter hover in the air, just above roof-level. Sure enough, it was Sugar piloting the thing.

Michaela bent over, scrambled up to the helicopter.

Leon waved, Lloyd did too.

Michaela and the man both waved back. After a few seconds, she walked around and got in the passenger side of the helicopter. The helicopter slowly turned and, as it turned, floated higher upward, then it moved out towards the pastureland behind the Bradford home.

The sound of the helicopter faded and Lloyd got an idea.

"So, Leon, I think I'll take you up on that ride in the Caddy another day."

Leon nodded and smiled a little. Do I have enough, thought Lloyd? Bill would say that he didn't, he knew that much. He thought about the medical examiner's office— what had they found out by now? If it's Walter's body—and if he stole the cattle—and Leon knows….Would they have had Walter killed? Michaela's a Baggott. Would have reason to hate Walter beyond the cattle thieving. Not poor old Leon, though. Surely not Leon.

As he walked back to his truck, it took everything he had not to turn around and cuff Leon and bring him in.

Lloyd made it about halfway down the long dirt drive from Leon's house back to the road before he met up with Bill's truck coming up the drive. He noticed someone in the passenger seat, someone small, the top of a head the only thing visible. He waved, and Bill pulled up alongside and Lloyd recognized Enid.

"We barking up the same tree, looks like," said Lloyd.

Bill winked and glanced over at Enid.

"Medical examiner identified the Parson's grove body as Walter Pound," said Bill. "Dental records. My sympathies—to you both," he added. "I know he was sorry but family is family."

They all sat quiet for a moment. Enid spoke first.

"It's Michaela what's done it," she said with authority, looked over at Lloyd.

"I think so, too," said Lloyd. "Just watched her hop on a helicopter with Sugar and whirl away. Lessons they called it."

Enid sat and listened whie the two men talked.

"I don't reckon Leon knows the first thing about any of this, but Michaela and that Sugar Burkson bastard—I'd bet the farm they did this together."

"For Michaela, motivation is there. The thievery and the family history."

"Don't forget the being crazy as a shithouse rat part," said Enid.

Lloyd smiled at Enid's comment.

"Enid, just thought of something," said Lloyd, raindrops beginning to tap on their truck hoods.

"Hoyt Baggott was Michaela's uncle, wasn't he?"

She nodded. "And my first cousin," she added.

"Well," said Bill, squinting at the dark gray sky. "Starting up again."

As the rain picked up, Lloyd waited impatiently for Bill to lay out their next moves. He told him to wait just off Bradford's property for Michaela's possible return by helicopter. Lay low and watch. Despite the rain angling in, Enid had not rolled up her window. Walters dead. Her man is dead. She seemed to be looking down as if there was something in her lap. Enid could have been someone, thought Lloyd, as Frank angled the truck into a three-point turn.

Acknowledgements

"The Tragedy of Carter Simms" appeared in *The Gambler*, as "The Tragedy of Warner Simms"; "The Cornish Cross" and "Love in Sahwoklee" appeared in *Emrys Journal*; "Death Comes for Noob Pierson" appeared in *Fiction365*, as "The Future Mrs. Crenshaw Asserts Herself to Good Effect"; "A Song for Enid Pound" appeared in *Madcap Review* and *Broad River Review*; "War in Sahwoklee" appeared in *Writers' Bloc*; "The Cone of Possibility" appeared in *Storyglossia*; "Jimmie & Lester" appeared in *Cowboy Jamboree*; "Tightrope Walkers" appeared in *BULL Fiction*; "The Tattler" appeared in *Deep South Magazine*; "Deek's Philosophies" appeared in *The Externalist*; "Unmentionables" appeared in *Paradise Review;* "The Patron Saint of Birds" appeared in *Plumb – A Journal of Appalachian Concerns,* as "Of Time and Virgins," and is based on an outline for a never-completed story by Breece D'J Pancake. "Counting by Mississippis" appeared in the collaborative text, *Mortality Birds.* "Wrong Kind of Rain" appeared in *Fried Chicken and Coffee.*

ABOUT THE AUTHOR

Steve Lambert was born in Louisiana and grew up in Florida. His writing has appeared in *Tampa review, Saw Palm*, *Chiron Review, New World Writing*, *The Pinch, Broad River Review, Louisiana Literature, Longleaf Review, Emrys Journal, BULL Fiction, Into the Void, Cortland Review*, and many other places. In 2015 he won third-place in *Glimmer Train*'s Very Short Fiction contest and in 2018 he won *Emrys Journal*'s Nancy Dew Taylor Poetry Prize. He is the recipient of four Pushcart Prize nominations and was a Rash Award in Fiction finalist. Interviews with Lambert have appeared in print, on podcasts, and public radio. He is the author of the poetry collections *Heat Seekers* (2017) and *The Shamble* (2021), the chapbook *In Eynsham* (2020), and the fiction collection *The Patron Saint of Birds* (originally published in 2020). His novel, *Philisteens*, was released in 2021. The collaborative fiction text, *Mortality Birds*, written with Timothy Dodd, appeared in 2022, as the first title from Southernmost Books. He and his wife live in Northeast Florida.

www.ingramcontent.com/pod-product-compliance
Lightning Source LLC
Chambersburg PA
CBHW041157150726
48006CB00016B/2016